Every Savage Can Reproduce

Pride and Prejudice-inspired Science Fiction

by

ENID WILSON

To

Debra Anne, Basia, Mihaela, Sylwia, Lisette, Linnea, Phia, Lucy, Lydia, Romi, Geri, Ruth, Paula, Hugo, Danielle, Karen and other readers who have helped shape the story plots throughout the years!

Enid Wilson loves sexy romance. Her writing career began with a daily newspaper, writing educational advice for students. She then branched out into writing marketing materials and advertising copy.

Enid's novels, *Bargain with the Devil* has been ranked in the top 50 best-selling historical romances on Amazon USA, *Really Angelic* in the top 30 best-selling Regency romances on Amazon Canada, *My Darcy Mutates* in the top 21 romantic short stories on Amazon UK and *Fire and Cross* in the top 39 British mysteries on Amazon.

Enid loves to hear from her readers. You can contact her at enid.wilson28@yahoo.com.au or www.steamydarcy.com

Cover design by Lavender C
First published 2011

Chapter One

"Children Are Not For Everyone"
– the Genesis Department, 3818

The tall, blond man wore a dark blue X-bio space suit fitted to his masculine body. He smoothed the fabric over his chest and thighs, then pushed his invitation card into the key slot. The door slid open, and an invigorating fresh scent blossomed around him. He drew in a long, deep breath and entered Love Your Mate's Capsule UR1.

A red haired woman turned away from the snake-shape vision pocket and acknowledged his presence, waved at a screen on the wall.

The capsule blasted off immediately.

The couple stood in silence for several minutes, gazing at each other until the horizon outside indicated that they had left Planet Earth.

Taking off her yellow i-techno space suit and the wig, the woman revealed a mass of chocolate brown curly hair under the disguise. Following her, the man took off his wig, revealing his dark, wavy hair.

"Thank you for coming, Mr. Darcy," the woman said.

"My pleasure, Miss Bennet," Fitzwilliam Darcy replied calmly, though his emotions were in turmoil. He had been stunned to receive a secret message from Elizabeth Bennet, requesting a meeting at one of the most infamous capsules in the Planet. These illegal establishments existed solely as a way for men and women to indulge in prohibited sexual activities, away from the hounding eyes of the Military Intelligence Agency, commonly referred to as the MIA.

Darcy had first met Elizabeth through his best friend, Charles Bingley, six months prior. Since then, he had been captivated by her compassionate, intelligent and lively character. She was different from any of the women he knew, never fawning over him or praising him to the sky because of his wealth and position. But he had not acted on his desire for her, nor had he asked her out. As one of the closest relatives of the newly selected Queen Immortal, the existing ruler of Planet Earth, he had to be scrupulously careful about those with whom he associated.

He had a lot to consider, especially when it concerned someone below his class. Planet Earth had adopted rigid class system since the apocalypse that had occurred fifty years earlier. Darcy's mother came from the Noble class, the second most important social stratum in the Planet. His father came from the Gentry class, one class below. Elizabeth's family, however, left a great deal to be desired. She was the second-eldest daughter of five. Although Mr. Bennet came from the same class as Darcy's father, Elizabeth's mother came from the Merchant class, yet another level below. Darcy had also witnessed the unruly behaviour of her younger sisters, which made him hesitant to associate with most of her family.

But the illicit nature of this rendezvous, and the promise of enjoying hours of this alluring woman about whom he had fantasised for months, had prompted his decision to come for today's meeting. For once, he was willing to forget his position in society, and seize the moment.

"Won't you have a seat?" Elizabeth said. The capsule was lit with a dim, soothing green light. A huge bed occupied one side, and a loveseat with a coffee table occupied another.

There was a glass door, leading to a luxuriously furnished bathroom. One could recline on the bed and watch as the other person took a shower or bath, as the partition and bathtub were made of cloudless steel, a transparent material.

Darcy had heard that the illegal mating capsules were full of promising gadgets, including endless supplies of mechanised condoms, vibrators, food with aphrodisiac properties, performance-enhancing drugs, edible body paints and mating aides. If someone could imagine it, these capsules offered it. Projections of erotic fantasies could be ordered on demand. Even the hiring of men or women to conduct gay, lesbian or multiple-partner games was commonplace.

But Darcy was not interested in any of those. He had come purely for her.

Taking a few slow steps, he chose to sit on the loveseat.

She did not come to sit by him, but remained standing near the bed.

"I have a proposal for you," Elizabeth said.

Darcy raised his eyebrows, and waited for her to continue.

"I want to have your baby."

His eyes widened. *She's one hell of a hussy!*

"By sperm donation," she clarified quickly.

"What?" It was the most outrageous proposition he had encountered. Even before his aunt became the Planet's ruler, many women had wanted to become his mistress or wife, for the money, position and power he could bring. No woman had ever come right out to ask him to father a child for her; and yet this woman wanted his sperm, but not him. Was she not interested in him as a lover, at all?

"Two months ago, I applied to the Reproduction Committee to have a baby by you, but they rejected my application, stating that the proposed father was unsuitable."

"Unsuitable? How?" Darcy couldn't believe it. He would have thought himself to be highly suitable, fit to father any woman's child.

"Mr. Wickham and Mr. Collins handed down the decision to me but they refused to explain further." She grimaced. "They said that the government didn't need to give a reason."

"Two of the least intelligent men in the Planet! I will check into it for you."

"There's no need. I already know it."

"Really? What is it?"

Her gaze darkened, and she hesitated. "Charles warned me that you're against the Committee. Can I trust you with what I've found out?"

"You should have heard enough about me to know that I'm against most of the strict laws imposed by the Queen."

"Ah yes – your aunt, the former Lady Catherine de Bourgh, now Catherine the Immortal."

"So, what did you find out? Why was I deemed unsuitable to father your child?"

"I hacked into the Committee's artificial intelligence centre. According to the record, you're engaged to the Queen Immortal's daughter. Your sperm is not to be bestowed upon any other women through the Committee."

"But that's absurd! I've never been engaged to Anne, and I've no intention of ever being engaged to her."

"So you're willing to gift your sperm to me?" Elizabeth asked, her face brightening.

He rose and paced around the capsule for a restless minute, then approached her. "Not so fast. Why did you want me to father your baby?"

She craned her neck to look up at him. Drawing a deep breath, she replied, "I am 21 years old now. I must start the process if I want to have more than one child."

Under the new laws introduced by the Queen Immortal, women in the Gentry class could only bear children before the age of 25, and had to apply through the Reproductive Committee. In order to improve the genetic composition of the people of the Planet, women could only apply to have a child by a man they knew from their own class or higher. The autocratic Queen believed that the higher the social stratum, the better their character. There had been protests against the law but they died down soon, after some violent suppression.

"Yes, but why me?"

"You're the most intelligent man I've ever known."

Darcy thought smugly. *She likes me!*

"And you're a better man than the others I've known so far." She paused, bit her lip and continued, "But, to tell you the truth, I've been hesitating for quite a while about this."

"Hesitating? Why?" Darcy could see no reason why any woman would fail to want him. He was the one who should be hesitant about having a baby with her.

"When you arrived at Hertfordshire, you looked down on most of us. You're arrogant and have a selfish disdain of others. You treat people with contempt and don't seem to care about them, if they're from a different class. But I'm sure, with my sole influence, that my child won't develop the same character faults that you exhibit. Still, it took me weeks of struggle to reach that decision and put you down on the application."

Darcy sucked in a deep breath. "My faults are grave indeed, as you describe them! And yet you nominate me as the father of your child, without even bothering to consult me first."

"There is no need to consult. The new law said that I could name anyone I knew. And what is it to you? You are required to have your sperm stored in the national storage facility, like all the upper-class men in the Planet. You'll only lose a small quantity of sperms. I was quite sure you would be happy about it. If you're anything like Catherine the Immortal, who wants to dominate and control our society, you must want to father as many children as possible, in the Planet, by farming out your genes. But after I was turned down by the Committee and learned about the reason, I knew I had been wrong about you."

"So you admit that you are in the wrong?"

"Only that you haven't yet bestowed your sperm upon anyone yet, through the Committee." Elizabeth frowned and continued, "I then reconsidered other candidates. But Mr. Collins is still too stupid. Mr. Hurst is still too lazy. Bingley is from the Merchant class. He's not allowed to have children. Anyway, Jane and he seem to have accepted their situation happily. I'll not upset their relationship with my own quest. And Mr. Wickham is..."

"You take an eager interest in that man!"

"I do not. I only analysed the situation. But you know very well why I can't apply for him."

"He's from the Working class and so, of course, he is not allowed to sire a child, either."

Elizabeth hesitated before continuing. "He's...In any event, after reconsidering the other candidates, I still adjudged you to be the most suitable. Since you are half Noble, half Gentry, you're not restricted by the law, and can choose to impregnate any woman you want. That is why I sent you an invitation. And you came, so that must mean that there is a chance I can persuade you to agree to my scheme. If you don't, I'll have to cross you out altogether and find another man."

Darcy's temper flared. *Cross me out? Find another man? Have a baby with another man? No!* "I'm nothing like my aunt," he corrected her firmly. "I don't – and won't – boost my ego by fathering enough children to fill the Planet."

The scowl on Elizabeth's face deepened. "So you're going to refuse me? Damn! I've gone about this all the wrong way. I suppose I should have kept my mouth shut, or told you how ardently I admire and love you. But I detest any sort of dishonesty."

"No, you wouldn't have gotten your own way by flattering me with words, either. And I won't donate my sperm to you. I can, however, be tempted by something else." Darcy walked one step closer, effectively trapping her between his body and the wall. Raising his fingers, he traced a path down her cheek, neck and shoulder, then slowly over the slope of her breast "I would be happy to have a child with you, but by natural means only."

Elizabeth's breath became shallow and her body shivered. "But I don't even like you!"

"Your body likes me." His fingers turned the caress into a slow kneading of her breasts.

Elizabeth trembled under his ministrations, her legs growing weak.

He recognised her desire. "See? Your nipples welcome my caress."

"That's just a physical response."

"It's quite a good start."

"Insemination is more scientific with a sperm donation, resulting in a higher success rate of conception," Elizabeth argued breathlessly in a last-ditch effort to persuade him to do things her way.

"It's more enjoyable with natural conception, and yields a higher satisfaction rate."

"Man and his carnal lust!"

"Not just man. And there's nothing wrong with that. We're made to fit into each other. Only my aunt wishes to interfere with the Lord's command and encourage artificial conception and other crazy laws."

Elizabeth frowned. "We'll do it just this one time?"

"No. We can't guarantee that you'll conceive in a single night, and I won't be satisfied with just one time," Darcy replied. "Spend three years with me. I may give you three babies, if we practise every day."

"Three years! That's far too long to be saddled with you."

He glared at her. *Such a shrew! But I've a good way to keep your mouth shut.* He lowered his mouth and kissed her hard, while his hands fondled her body. After a few minutes of sucking her lips, he ended the scorching kiss and added, "Or you can cross me off your list and seek some other man."

He walked away from her and stretched out slowly on the bed. With his hands beneath his chin, he lay on his stomach as he gazed at her with a challenging glint. Judging by her response to his initial kiss, he felt confident that she would give in to his demand.

"Arrogant man!" She moved away from the bed, swearing beneath her breath, then stopped. "How can I be certain that you wouldn't interfere with my upbringing of the children?"

"Ah, my character faults! Are you so certain that they're not hereditary? Do you want me to go through some psychological or medical examination first, to make sure that I won't pass along some defective gene to our child? Or are you willing to trust your instincts, since you say that I'm the best man you've known so far." He winked at her. "Your options would seem to be limited."

Elizabeth's eyes flashed and her fists clenched.

He continued calmly, "I can sign a contract that assures you sole custody of the children when you have fulfilled the three years' obligation."

She paced closer, looking down at him. "Let's start with a one year fixed contract and a two year option," Elizabeth proposed, her eyes narrowed in a calculated glint.

"Fine."

"I'll order the capsule to go round now."

But Darcy stopped her from waving at the console and pulled her down. When she tumbled onto him, he rolled over and trapped her underneath him.

Elizabeth panted as his hard, strong body pressed against hers. She looked hot and flustered.

"Why waste the mating capsule? Let's start," Darcy urged.

"Start?"

"Let's make a baby, Elizabeth! I've heard a lot about these mating capsules. Indeed, if you had asked me to meet you at some other place, I wouldn't have come, and you wouldn't have had a chance to make your proposition. But now, as things stand, we've reached an agreement and we have a whole night here." He smiled. "What could be better?"

Elizabeth squirmed, trying to move away from his body, but her movements only caused their bodies to rub together. "Perhaps I should order a medical check first, before we sign any contract. I wouldn't want to catch any diseases from you."

He laughed. "You can check me out for yourself. I assure you, I'm scrupulously clean and exceptionally fit." He lowered his head and traced the tip of his tongue across her lips. Then he slipped his tongue into her sweet mouth, and was gratified when she returned the overture by suckling his tongue.

His hands moved to unzip her skin-tight body suit, baring her gorgeous breasts for exploration. The touch of her soft skin electrified him, leaving him sizzling hot and acutely aroused. He pushed her body suit further down, and she shifted cooperatively, helping him. His mouth left hers and followed his hands, to worship her twin peaks and her navel. When he tugged the suit completely off of her, exposing her sex to his blazing mouth and hands, he felt as if he might come at any second.

"Wait. I want to see you too," Elizabeth whispered, hesitantly.

Darcy smiled, glad that she was coming around to his idea of love making. He let her help him unzip his body suit and push it away.

Raising her body, Elizabeth began kissing him, moving from shoulder to torso, down his abdomen to his belly button. Growing more aggressive, she pushed him down to lie on the bed, then hovered above him, her slender hands seeming to explore every part of his body.

Darcy closed his eyes, savouring her passionate response. Amid the haze of heightened sensation, he felt her urge his arms above his head, and he complied.

Click!

Click!

Opening his eyes, he found his hands handcuffed to the headboard of the bed.

"What are you doing?" Annoyance and confusion shaded toward alarm as he tried to pull himself free. The handcuffs seemed to consist of a transparent magnetic field. He couldn't see them, but they bound his hands tightly. He couldn't slip out of them, nor could he wrench them open.

"Sorry!" Elizabeth gave him a peck on the cheek, turned away to secure his ankles, one to each of the bedposts, despite his fierce struggling.

Darcy was spread-eagled on the bed, naked and vulnerable. He looked up at her, panting in apprehension. *What does she intend to do to me?*

Voting Options

1) Elizabeth performs an experiment on Darcy

2) Elizabeth steals something from Darcy

3) Darcy turns the table on Elizabeth √

4) Elizabeth hands Darcy to someone else

CHAPTER TWO

"What do you want? Release me immediately!" Darcy cried out angrily. He pulled at the invisible handcuffs with force, but they didn't budge. He had never been placed in such a vulnerable position before, naked and trussed, at the mercy of a woman half his size.

She stood beside the bed, gazing down at him with an infuriating express of calm. "I still think my method will be easier, Mr. Darcy. We won't need to... fake anything when we make this baby. In fact, we won't need to see each other ever again, after this one time. I've brought along a medical freezer to store your sperm. You'll only need to... umh... do it for me once."

Elizabeth sat by him on the edge of the mattress, not bothering to gather up the body suit to cover her naked body. She was still overheated from the effort of subduing him and tying his ankles to the end of the bed. Only the element of surprise had made it possible. Without it, he would have proved too strong.

She had never touched the body of a naked man before. During the struggle, she had repeatedly found his lower body pressing to hers in a way that was too close for comfort. Flustered now, she diverted her glance to his feet instead. *His toes look quite adorable! In fact, he looks extremely handsome, with or without a stitch of clothing...* She gave herself a mental shake. *Stop it, Lizzy! Concentrate on the matter at hand.*

She shifted her weight, intending to fetch the freezer, but he began to argue. "I didn't agree for you to take my sperm, you know. It's a theft if you do it without my consent. Do you want me to drag you into court afterwards? Do you want our children to be born under a shadow of animosity?"

Elizabeth turned to glare at him. "You agreed to father my child. Why do you have to be so stubborn about the method?"

"Haven't you read the research studies that assert that babies who are the result of natural conception and two-parent families are emotionally more balanced?"

"Tell that to your aunt! She banned the people of the Gentry class and below from having sex before marriage when she became the Genesis Director, twenty years ago. Now that she has become Queen Immortal, she even dictates how we can have children. I think she's insane! And I don't believe in those research studies you cite. Humans have used natural conception and had two-parent families for thousands of years, and you can see what that did for them! We still have emotionally unbalanced people -- people like your aunt – who think they can control the world."

"I agree with you about my aunt. That's why I don't choose to be associated with her. It's the media, the government, and even the religions that produce greedy or power-hungry people, from time to time. But, Elizabeth, I'm not like that. I'm just a normal man who wants to have an ordinary family one day." His tone softened. "Although I haven't thought about the timing yet, your proposition seems to fit well. You're smart and compassionate. I saw how you took care of Jane when she was sick at Netherfield. I'm truly happy that you chose me to father your child...but I want to raise our children together. I can help you shape their character."

She recoiled. "You? Shape their character? Didn't I mention that you're arrogant and unfeeling?"

"Arrogance is having pretensions to a superior importance. I didn't think I'm pretentious at all. Is it such a crime that I believe that my heritage, my wealth and my body are things to be proud of? I didn't speak with most of the people in Hertfordshire, but it wasn't because I'm unfeeling. I'm just not good at conversing with people I don't know!"

"You're a man of sense and education. Why should you find it hard to recommend yourself to strangers?"

"I don't know. Maybe you can teach me how, in the future." He was pleading now. "Elizabeth, release me. We can do this amicably and naturally. Why do you want to pursue such a clinical method?"

Elizabeth was torn. Initially, she had been worried that she would need to persuade him to agree to father her child. After all, she was a nobody, with neither wealth nor connections, as compared to him. Frankly, she was surprised that he was agreeing so readily. And she was even more stunned to find that the method of conception had become the main point of contention.

She had not come with a plan to tie him up. The mating capsule was a novel venture for her. She had come aboard nearly an hour early, and had explored the place, as a way to calm her nerves. That was when she had discovered the invisible magnetic handcuffs and other strange apparatus in a drawer near the headboard, along with the mating capsule's user manual. Caught off guard when he suddenly demanded to make the baby by having sex, she had panicked and reached for the handcuffs, tying him up to slow things down a bit. His mouth and body did such strange things to her that she wasn't sure who she distrusted more – Darcy or herself...

Seeing that she was distracted and lost in thought, Darcy moved his right thumb to press the signet on the ring he wore on his little finger, activating the mechanism within it. Rays of stellar flare beamed down his hand to the wrist, disrupting the magnetic hold on his wrist, freeing his right arm.

Elizabeth cried out in alarm, but Darcy moved like a panther, wrapped his arm around her waist and holding her against him as he twisted to free his other hand.

Elizabeth scream again as he held her tightly against his body. She struggled, but he was bigger and stronger. Imprisoning her with his left arm, he raised his right hand and angled it so that the stellar flare opened the restraints around his ankles. With this accomplished, he deactivated the current and rolled his big body on top of her.

"What should I do with you now?" he asked slowly, his gaze dark and menacing.

Elizabeth shuddered. He did not sound exactly cold or angry when he murmured, but the eager lust she had first seen in his face was gone. *What will he do with me?*

She licked her dry lips. "Perhaps...perhaps we should simply forget about the whole thing, as we can't agree on the method of conception. Please get off of me. I'll get the capsule back to Earth and seek another candidate."

"Let you go, when I have you naked under me? No way!" He raised her hands over her head and held them there by gathering her wrists in one of his left hand. Then he rubbed her lips with his right thumb. "Ah, but now that you have put the idea of conceiving a child into my head, I can't be dismissed so easily." Reaching to the side, he pulled the bedside drawer open farther and searched through the other gadgets there.

"Condom...vibrator...whip...feather... Ah, here's what I want." He lifted out a pair of traditional handcuffs made of metal, and turned the tables on her by cuffing her hands to the headboard.

Elizabeth squirmed and wiggled, pulling against the handcuffs as she growled angrily, "You can't have sex with me like this. It's non-consensual! It's rape!"

He brushed the displaced curls from her forehead and asked, "Why are you so afraid of making love with me?"

"I am afraid of making love to any man. What woman wouldn't be? I am from the Gentry class. Do you think me foolish, or unschooled? I have listened to the lectures from the Genesis Department. You call it 'making love,' but they have made it clear that it's hard and painful work – work which the Noble men and women endure for the greater good of the Planet."

"Rubbish from my aunt. Making love is enjoyable, so long as you are physically attracted to the partner. It is an act that connects two people most intimately." Gently, he grazed his knuckles over her face.

Elizabeth panted. "You've done it many times?"

"Not too many, but enough to know it can be enjoyable. I confess that this will be my first time in a very long while. Shall I show you?" he invited, and gazed down at her.

She shook her head and tried again to struggle free. "No. I still prefer artificial insemination. Don't force me!"

He sat up, straddling her lower body, and smiled encouragingly. "You'll change your mind."

Using the feather, he brushed it lightly along a path from her earlobe to her cheekbone, then along her tense jaw and down to her slender neck. His mouth and tongue followed, sensitizing her skin. Next, he lowered the feather to her glorious breasts, toying with her nipples, stroking and teasing them until they gathered and hardened in response. His tongue twirled around each peak in turn, dampening the aureoles, which turned a deep red.

The feather slid lower along Elizabeth's abdomen and lingered at her navel, as his mouth progressed from licking to suckling the nipples, as if trying to drink the juice from each delicious cherry peak. He rubbed his lower body and rampant arousal against her hips and her sex, grinding against her smooth skin and her crisp bush, tempting her to relax the muscles of her legs.

Elizabeth gasped at the electrifying sensations created by his tongue, mouth and body, and by the wicked feather. She hadn't known she could feel such incredible things in so many places in her body. His touch warmed her blood and invigorated her cells, making her want to jump up and dance with joy. She moaned and arched her body, closing her eyes to savour his stroking. Her muscles trembled and shivered.

Darcy lowered his body further. He had one of her legs imprisoned still as he kissed her belly button, then flicked the feather lower, to her apex. He used his other hand to part her legs more widely. The feather tickled at her secret lips, tracing the line where they joined, lightly at first, but soon with more insistence.

The soft touch sent shock waves through her body. She screamed in startled ecstasy, and her body jerked in response, bucking sharply against his abdomen in the process.

He drew in a deep breath and said, "Such a tigress!" Tossing the feather aside, he grasped her free leg, pushing it wider still, and lowered his mouth to kiss her folds. He nipped and licked her secret lips, and was gratified to find her drenched with juice. Giving her no time to recoil, he suckled her fervently, whirling her into a dark vortex of desire.

The taste of her moist skin was intoxicating, and her womanly scent taunted him. He was like an addict who couldn't get enough of her essence. When he thrust his tongue into her entrance, she cried out loud and reached climax instantly, her muscles convulsing and contracting for a long, writhing minute. Afterwards, she went limp.

He gazed down at her porcelain body, which was now glowing crimson. Elizabeth was panting hard, her eyes half closed, her pretty mouth half-open. He wanted to thrust into her core, there and then, and bring her to another climax...but he hesitated.

If I have sex with her now and make her pregnant, will she disappear with my child? Should I wait until we have signed a contract? Or should I make her mine now, addicting her to my love-making before I give her a child? Would it be morally manipulative to attempt to use my sexual power to tie her to me? Nonsense. It is simply sensible, given that she was perfectly prepared to steal my sperm while I was handcuffed.

His mind was made up. Raising his body, he rolled a condom onto his hard shaft, and unlocked the handcuffs. Elizabeth lay lax in the aftermath of her climax, letting him do whatever he wanted. He settled over her and stroked her breasts, toying with her nipples as he began to press gently, rhythmically against her apex. Soon, he felt her body begin to rouse and response to the seductive pressure. She entwined her arms around his body, caressing his back, smoothing her fingertips up and down his spine as she returned his kiss with increasing passion. Her legs parted instinctively to allow him to settle more naturally between her. She squeezed and relaxed her thighs again and again, clearly enjoying the contact with his body.

He ended a sizzling kiss and drew back just far enough to whisper softly, "Do you want me, Elizabeth?"

She turned her mouth to seek his lips and said, "Don't stop!"

"Is that a yes?"

"Yes, I want you. Don't stop."

Darcy smiled triumphantly and guided her legs up to wrap around his waist. Positioning his manhood, he began to push against her tight entrance, slowly, inexorably. Inch by inch, he parted her grasping muscles...until he reached an unexpected barrier. Her maidenhead.

"Dear God. You're still a virgin?" He stopped his movement and drew in several deep breaths.

"Of course. I'm from the Gentry class. We are not allowed to have sex."

"But many people break that law. I thought..." He panted, trying to control himself. "I should stop now."

"No!" Her arms tightened around him. "Don't stop. I want you!" She wanted to taste that incredible feeling of ecstasy again. If she was going to defy government law and had this man's baby illegally, she might as well enjoy it.

"But..."

Desperate to prevent him, she grabbed his buttocks and tried to pull him down onto her body.

Her tiny hands on the cheeks of his buttocks, and the prick of her nails as they gripped his vulnerable flesh, shattered his control. He thrust into her with force, to the hilt.

Elizabeth cried out in a piercing scream.

Darcy stopped to savour the movement, then lowered his head to kiss her damp forehead. "Just breathe, Elizabeth. It'll get better, once your body get used to me."

A solitary tear rolled down her cheek. "It's true."

"What's true?"

"What they told us. It really is hard work that needs to be endured," she said accusingly, her lower lip trembling as unshed tears shone in her eyes.

He kissed her gently and said, "Trust me. It's not hard work. Soon, you will feel the same ecstasy you experienced before."

Soon he started thrusting, at a snail's pace at first, allowing her untried muscles to accustom themselves to his thick cock.

Elizabeth still found it painful, like being torn apart by him. But she wanted to relish the same feeling she had felt when he kissed her sex. Bravely, she responded by arching her body up to greet him, thrust by thrust. Before long, she felt less pain, and then the first stirrings of pleasure.

Her responsive movements urged him on. He pushed into her again and again. The sound of their moaning, and the meshing of the bodies, created a mating melody inside the capsule. They climbed higher and higher together, until they reached their peak, convulsed and cried out, bursting into flame in unison.

After a long while, Darcy withdrew from Elizabeth's warm body, disposed of the condom, and drew her lax body to sprawl on top of him. He caressed her hips and whispered sweet words into her ear...

Suddenly, their tranquillity was interrupted.

The capsule shook, rousing them from the lethargy of their lovemaking.

"What is it?" Elizabeth raised her head, looking around in alarm.

Darcy turned to the vision pocket. Outside, it was still dark, and the stars shone brightly. "I'm not sure."

Another tremor occurred, sharper this time. Darcy sprung up from the bed and stood in front of the vision pocket, while Elizabeth waved at the console.

"Damn, we're being attacked!" Darcy exclaimed. The capsule, continuing to shake, began to move at a faster speed, zigging and zagging. Darcy and Elizabeth hurried to don their body suits.

"Does this capsule have a protective shield?" he asked.

"Let me check." She touched the screen on the wall. "It's on already."

"What's the emergency plan? Can they beam us back to Earth?" He moved to stand next to Elizabeth, looking at the console.

"There's no beaming facility in the capsule. They didn't want the government to hack into the system and beam up agents. It only has an automatic firearm-avoidance device and a radar cruise control. It's taking us to the nearest safe planet," she said.

"Does it show who's hot on our tail?"

She checked the screen. "It's one of the spaceships from the MIA!"

"Military Intelligence Agency? Damn. Are there any weapons onboard the capsule?"

"There are all sorts of strange items in the drawers by the headboard and here. But I don't think they're weapons."

Darcy went through all the items. "Whips, chains and belts. Useless mating aides. No real firearm."

Abruptly, a blast struck the console, and the computer system read-out darkened. The capsule dropped attitude dramatically. Darcy grabbed Elizabeth by the waist and rolled with her to the floor, where he held onto the leg of the bed.

Voting Options

1) *Military Intelligence Agency (MIA) spaceship captures the capsule, and Darcy and Lizzy are arrested*

2) The capsule crashes onto an unknown planet, and Darcy and Lizzy are captured by its occupants √

3) *Darcy and Lizzy escape the pursuit of the MIA's spaceship and return safely to Earth*

CHAPTER THREE

After endless minutes of freefall, the capsule shook with a huge impact. Darcy was thrown by the force, losing his hold on the leg of the bed. As he rolled, he held tightly onto Elizabeth, sheltering her, until his head crashed into a corner and he lost consciousness.

When the shaking of the capsule finally stopped, Elizabeth tried to catch her breath. She realised that Darcy was limp in her embrace, and felt a thrill of fear.

"Mr. Darcy?" she said a few times; but he did not respond to her call. She pushed his shoulder, rolling him slightly away from where he rested against her, and saw that he had cuts on his head and shoulder. "Dear God, don't die on me!" She checked his pulse, and was relieved to find that he was still breathing. Trying harder, she managed to slip her body out from under him.

Climbing unsteadily to her feet, she assessed the damage inside the capsule and looked for something she could use to bandage his wounds. A compartment on the side of the computer console had sprung open, its door hanging askew. When she examined it, she found that it contained an emergency first aid kit. She treated Darcy's wounds as best she could, and managed to stop the bleeding. She also used the medical scanner she found to check his vital signs. He seemed largely unharmed, except for his continued loss of consciousness. As he was too heavy for her to move, she took the pillow and sheet from the bed and made him as comfortable as possible on the floor.

"Mr. Darcy, can you hear me?" she asked a few more times, but he still did not respond.

Concerned, Elizabeth checked the capsule again. Except for the crippled console and the objects that had been thrown around, there seemed to be no major damage to its structure. She looked out from the snake-shaped window and saw that it was very dark outside; indeed, she couldn't see a thing. She wouldn't venture out until it was brighter, or at least until Mr. Darcy woke up.

With a sigh, she settled herself beside him, and thought about their acquaintance.

When she had first learned that he was Queen Catherine's nephew, she'd taken an instant dislike to him. The Queen was a dictator. It seemed likely that her nephew would be equally domineering, egotistical and haughty. His initial behaviour at the Meryton Assembly had certainly reinforced her belief. He had been arrogant, condescending and unsociable, not talking to or socializing with the locals. But during her stay at Charles's estate of Netherfield, when Jane was ill, she had found Darcy to be smart, knowledgeable and sensible instead. They had engaged in some interesting conversations, And she had later observed and heard enough to know that he held very different ideas about society from those of his aunt.

When Jane and she talked about their plans for having children, Jane admitted she loved Charles and was prepared not to have children by marrying into the Merchant class to become his wife. Elizabeth had been more proactive, deciding it was time to take the chance and apply to the Reproduction Committee. Before she filled out the application form, she made a list of all the men she knew, from young to old, and evaluated their strengths and weaknesses. Mr. Darcy added up the best. He was tall and handsome, and he looked healthy and fit. He was also intelligent. She hoped her child would inherit those attributes. Of course, she understood the erratic nature of genetics. Her child might inherit all the bad elements from both of them; but she would hope for the best and give it a go.

It was a shock when her application was turned down and the Committee recommended, instead, that she utilise sperm from Mr. Collins. She couldn't stand the man. He was the Queen Immortal's commander, a "yes" man for the Queen, without opinion or backbone. He looked and acted stupid. She would rather go without than burden her child with such a father.

She had thought, originally, that Mr. Darcy might have turned down her application. She knew that the Committee sometimes contacted the nominated father, to ascertain his willingness. Most of the time, however, the Committee simply allocated the sperm in storage as they wished. She had thought that Darcy might have despised her for her audacity in daring to name him as the nominated father, since she was a country nobody with no fortune or connection. But the reality had turned out quite differently. He hadn't turned her down. In fact, he wanted more than she was willing to give. But now that they had done the deed...

NO! He used a condom just now! Elizabeth suddenly remembered. Through her haze of desire, she had allowed him to make love to her in the natural way. But why had he used a condom? Damn the man! It was cheating.

He claimed that he wanted to make the baby the natural way and stay together for three years. Why did he do that? Was he angry because I handcuffed him? What if he just wanted to enjoy some free sex, without the potential burden of a child?

She looked down at him, where he lay defenceless.

But he protected me just now, during the fall, she reasoned, *and injured himself. That wasn't the act of someone cold and unfeeling. Does he like me? His love-making was passionate. Perhaps he did. But what if he changes his mind now? Perhaps I didn't satisfy him, being a virgin.* She sighed. *Still, he whispered sweet words to me after we made love. Oh, I'm so confused. Maybe I should just do it my way, now that he's unconscious.*

Elizabeth paced around the capsule, looking at the senseless man. Frowning, she retrieved the medical freezer she had brought along. *It's unethical to steal his sperm when he's not aware of it. Should I not be thinking about how to get us safely back to Earth, rather than making a baby.*

She left his side and checked on the console. She was very good at software, but repairing hardware damage was beyond her. After punching a few keys and trying to unscrew the panel without success, she gave up and paced around the capsule again. She knocked on every panel, looking for more unexpected compartments, but didn't find any.

As she neared the bed, she noticed the intimate items strewn around the capsule, and saw the packets of condoms.

Her expression darkened, and she stalked back to where Darcy lay sprawled. *He started this! He had sex with me, knowing full well that I wanted to conceive, and yet he used a condom. We agreed to have a baby, and he didn't do what he said he would. My mind is made up. I'll do it my way!*

She bit her lips and then, with trembling fingers, pulled the bed sheet aside and unzipped his body suit. When she bared his manhood, she stole a guilty glance at it, debating what to do.

Gathering her courage, she tentatively brushed her fingers along his length, from base to tip. The texture was surprisingly velvety and smooth. She stroked it again, more firmly, but her ministrations weren't enough to make it spring to life.

What next? She had read before that a woman could use her mouth to excite a man's body, but she had certainly never done such a thing. Would it work? Still too shy to look at his shaft, she closed her eyes, bent low over him and inhaled deeply.

She was greeted by the enticing scent of sex from their previous lovemaking. Hesitantly, drawn to him, Elizabeth extended her tongue and bent even closer, gingerly touching him.

At first, she licked the wrong place, touching his pubic hair, judging by the rough bushy texture, so she put out her hands and felt her way. Her questing fingers found his hip and gravitated blindly toward the centre of his body, where she finally encountered his shaft.

Pulse quickening, she tried to distract her mind from the image of his potent body. Cradling his cock in her hand, she started licking him, and felt it growing, becoming bigger and longer. But after several minutes of brushing its surface with her tongue, she still couldn't make him come. And so, debating furiously with herself, she opened her eyes and boldly decided to take him fully in her mouth.

It was a strange sensation. He was hard and yet soft. He seemed to grow and stretch. He tasted salty and musky; and accepting him so intimately made her whole body feel hot.

Suddenly, his legs moved.

Elizabeth looked up, startled. He was moving. *Damn, he must be waking up!* She immediately released him from her mouth, afraid that he would wake to find her in such a compromising situation. Hastily, she tugged the bed sheet over to cover him again. Then she scrambled to her feet and went to stand in front of the vision pocket, pretending to enjoy the view while calming herself. That was when she saw a cruiser flying directly toward them.

We have company! Is that good news or bad?

Behind her, she could hear Darcy as his moans, soft at first, gained intensity. Concerned, she tore her gaze from the approaching cruiser and turned back toward him. She was startled to see that he had shifted onto his stomach and was now moving rhythmically, with the sheet bunched beneath him...

For a frozen instant, she struggled to make sense of the motion – and it dawned on her what she was seeing. She bolted toward him – but it was already too late. As she approached, the action of his hips quickened, and then he stiffened and cried out.

Tears of frustration stung her eyes. He had actually come, while her back was turned. *Damn my luck! What a wasted chance. But I can't do anything about it now. That cruiser isn't going to wait!* Fuming, she snatched a towel from the bathroom, cleaned Darcy up quickly, and tugged his body suit onto him as he squirmed slowly, not yet fully conscious, hindering her efforts more than he helped.

"Mr. Darcy, can you wake up? There's someone coming. Please, you must wake up!"

Darcy groaned. His head and shoulder ached. An extreme lethargy seemed to have claimed his body. But he heard the urgent pleas of a sweet voice. Turning, he focused on the woman speaking...and abruptly remembered the events of the day.

"What's wrong?"

"I've spotted a cruiser coming toward us. We need to be prepared."

"Damn, we have no weapons!"

"No, but I found a first aid kit, so I've hidden the scissors and knife. Let's hope we don't need to use them. Can you stand?"

He pulled himself up, with her help, just as the door of the capsule began to glow and melt in a violet ray of light. Darcy wrapped his arm protectively around Elizabeth and braced for the unknown.

A moment later, what was left of the door was pushed aside, and two heavily armed soldiers appeared in the opening, looking at them curiously.

"What have we got here? What a handsome couple! What are your names? Have you enjoyed the stay in the capsule?" the young woman of the pair asked cheerfully.

Before they could respond, the male officer said, "Why, Officer Woodhouse, don't speak so foolishly. Clearly, they are fugitives from Earth. Let us follow protocol."

"Captain Knightly, you're no fun at all. What's wrong with a bit of friendly...companionship?" Woodhouse responded.

Stepping forward, Elizabeth said, "I am Elizabeth Bennet, and this is my...friend, Fitzwilliam. We were attacked by the MIA." She waited for their reaction, hoping that the female officer's friendliness meant that Darcy and she would come to no harm. She had no intention of telling them Darcy's full name, as she didn't want them to know that he was a close relative of the unpopular Queen of Planet Earth.

"I'm Emma," the uniformed young woman stated. "Nice to meet you, Elizabeth! As to the MIA pursuit, we already know all about it. Only mating capsules chased by the MIA would be allowed to land here. We'll have cruisers chasing the MIA away."

"I don't understand. Are you saying that you represent...a safe house for people from the mating capsules?"

"You could say that."

"Where are we then? Can you help us get back to Planet Earth?"

"You're on Planet Hartfield. Our ancestors migrated here because they didn't like the crazy rules and pollution of Earth."

"Emma, the protocol!" Captain Knightley objected with a frown.

"Fine, fine, sir! We must observe the protocol, Elizabeth and Fitzwilliam, or my dear Captain Knightley will be very unhappy. That means that we will have to scan you, first, to see if you are genuine articles."

"What do you mean by that?" Darcy asked.

"We encounter MIA agents disguised as escapees, from time to time. We have to make sure you aren't trying to infiltrate our planet in order to bring in restrictive ideas or viruses." Emma explained.

Her partner prodded, "Emma, proceed with the protocol."

"Yes, my dear Captain," she said, and rolled her eyes at Knightley.

Taking a palm-sized device from her belt buckle, Emma shone it onto Darcy and Elizabeth, scanning each of them from head to toe. She then punched a few keys and read out the result to her captain. "OK, Elizabeth here has had two orgasms, and as has Fitzwilliam. The sexual satisfaction level was very high for Fitzwilliam and high for Elizabeth. They've used the feather, the handcuffs and a condom since coming aboard."

Both Elizabeth and Darcy turned bright red upon hearing Emma's words.

"Why did you scan us for such information?" Elizabeth asked.

"Most MIA personnel trying to infiltrate our planet do not actually use the features of the mating capsule. They are mainly officers from the Working Class, so they aren't allowed to have sex. We invented this sexometre to check whether the people who got shot down really are fugitives. The scanner can check your heartbeat, pulse, and sweat levels to analyse whether or not you have just had sex, and the level of satisfaction. It can also scan feathers, condoms, chains and whips for trace elements, to determine whether you have used them. I must congratulate you, Elizabeth. You seem to have made Fitzwilliam a very happy man. His rating shot through the roof." Emma grinned and winked at Elizabeth.

Elizabeth felt herself turn an even deeper shade of red. She glanced quickly at Darcy, and saw that he wore a puzzled look. "So, what now?" she asked Emma again.

"Well, you two will be quarantined here for fourteen days. We will come back to take you to town while our maintenance team will try to fix your capsule. It's part of the service we provide for the Love Your Mate, LYM, franchise from whom you hired this mating capsule."

"But why do we have to be quarantined? You just confirmed that we are fugitives."

"This was just an initial check-up. We'll be conducting a more in-depth investigation, sending your data to LYM to confirm your authenticity. It takes time to confirm whether you were really shot down or if you staged your freefall onto us. We also need to make sure you haven't brought in any viruses or germs from Earth. Tomorrow, we will bring you food and our vaccines."

"What are we supposed to do until then?" Elizabeth demanded.

Captain Knightly said seriously, "Just continue what you have been doing. If you are who you say you are, you hired this mating capsule in order to have sex. You now have at least two weeks in which to do it as many times as you like," He paused, before adding, "And don't think about running away. We have this capsule under surveillance. Officer Woodhouse, it's time for us to depart."

"Bye, Elizabeth! Bye, Fitzwilliam! Enjoy yourselves. I'll bring you more mating aides. Time will fly, with those on hand!" she said, and winked at them again.

Elizabeth blushed tomato-red and felt hot all through her body. Moving away from Darcy, she sank down weakly on the edge of the bed. "Fourteen days of sex? Are people crazy on this planet? Mr. Darcy, are you good at hardware repair? Maybe we can fix the console ourselves and leave earlier."

"No, I'm an agriculturalist. I'm not very good with computers."

"Damn! Well I guess we can always eat and chat. I hope Emma will bring a computer so that we can at least use the galaxynet. Jane will be worried if I don't return by tomorrow."

"I doubt whether Captain Knightley would do so. They are still not 100% convinced that we are not MIAs. I don't think they will allow us to contact anybody on Earth."

The two of them fell silent, brooding.

After several minutes, Darcy said, "There's one thing I don't understand, Elizabeth. May I ask you?"

"Sure. Fire away."

Darcy gazed at her and asked, "What did you do to me when I was unconscious?"

She replied innocently. "I bandaged your head and shoulder."

"You didn't try to...steal something from me?" He pointed to the medical freezer on the floor, near the pillow.

Elizabeth bit her lip and retorted, "Why did you use protection, when we made love?"

"I see. It was your revenge, then. So, were you successful? Shall I go and check the content of the freezer?"

"You haven't answered me."

He sighed. "We haven't signed a contract yet. How can I be sure you wouldn't just take off, if I got you pregnant?"

"If you felt that way about it, you should have waited to have sex with me until after we signed the contract. Insufferable man! I'm a gentlewoman of honour – "

" – who was willing to steal my bodily fluids while I was unconscious. Tell me, did you enjoy it?"

"Can we think about how to fix the computer, rather than this?"

"They said they would help us go, after two weeks. Why the hurry? After all, I heard what Officer Woodhouse said. Apparently there is still room for improvement, ways for me to make you more satisfied in bed than you were, to move your sexometre readings from high to very high. Shall we start practicing?"

"Dream on! I won't let you touch a strand of my hair again until the contract is signed." On that note, Elizabeth strode into the bathroom and slammed the door shut, intent on taking a shower to help herself cool down.

In her angry state, she totally forgot that the bathroom was transparent. Darcy reclined on the bed, savouring every moment as he watched her strip naked. Her breasts were bouncy, her hips curvaceous. Her voluptuous figure quickly turned him on. *Should I join her?*

Voting Options

1) *Darcy and Elizabeth wander away from the capsule, and one of them goes missing*

2) *Darcy's identity is known, and people from Planet Hartfield plan to use him as a bargaining chip* √

3) *MIA attacks Planet Hartfield*

CHAPTER FOUR

Inside the cruiser, Captain Knightley and Officer Woodhouse discussed their latest captives.

"What do you think of the new prisoners?" Knightley asked.

"Fitzwilliam is tall, dark and drop-dead gorgeous. I envy Elizabeth. I could think of plenty of ways to spend two weeks with him, if I wasn't otherwise engaged. She's very pretty, too, and quite friendly. A well-matched couple. I wonder why the MIA shot them down."

"MIA shoots down all capsules. You should know that, by now. And, Officer, I'm not asking you about the physical attributes of the inmates. I'm asking your opinion on whether they are genuine."

"Whyever wouldn't they be? The sexometre is usually pretty accurate."

"Your observation skills leave much to be desired. Didn't you notice the wigs on the floor?"

"What wigs?"

"There was a blond wig and a red one, among the things on the floor. That may well mean that the two inmates were disguised when they boarded the mating capsule."

"I was too busy being friendly, trying to get them to drop their guard. What's so significant about the possibility that they boarded the capsule under disguise? Most LYM patrons do that, to avoid MIA's surveillance."

"But Miss Bennet didn't tell us her lover's surname."

"What's so special about that, either? She may not even know it."

Knightley scowled. "Highly unlikely. They engaged in illegal activity together. There are risks involved, and Miss Bennet could, in fact, be an MIA agent in disguise. Fitzwilliam could be jailed, tortured or exiled for having illegal sex. Wouldn't it be recklessly and foolhardy not to know with whom you are dealing?"

"My dear Captain Knightley! Not everyone is as suspicious as you are. Perhaps they simply met on the street, lusted after each other, and hired a capsule for the night. What do they call that on Earth?"

"A one-night stand."

"Yes, a one-night stand. So, why bother with names? They may never see each other, after this."

"I doubt it. Didn't you notice how protective Fitzwilliam was toward Miss Bennet when we entered? His hands were clenched and his body tensed. He was ready to fight us, even though he had no weapons."

"How gallant! I wish someone would be willing to do that for me. Would you, George?"

"Don't bat your eyelashes. I'm used to your antics. And you're skilled at all kinds of combat, so you don't need my protection. How about the medical freezer? Did you at least see that?"

Emma rolled her eyes. "You seem to have scanners for eyes and a computer chip in your brain. How could you have noticed so many things in such a short time?"

"Years of training. Officer. You should work on doing that, too. Play less and work more."

"But that would make me a very dull Emma! Now enlighten me, sir – what is the significance of a medical freezer?"

"I couldn't say...yet. We'll know more, once we contact LYM and transfer the bio-data of the two fugitives to them."

"Maybe they plan to kidnap you, extract some of your genes, and clone a whole new Captain Knightley! If they do that, I'll demand that they create a more playful version of you," she said, and broke into giggles.

Knightley gave her a scowl, picked her up and walked into the armoury.

"You need to be court-marshalled, for making fun of your superior!" she screeched loudly, before cradling his head and kissed him soundly on the mouth.

"We shouldn't be doing this," he murmured, pressing her against the shelves of laser rifles. His hands smoothed over her body, taking off the body armour, the gun sling and the ammunition belt in the process.

Emma was more impatient. She unzipped his space trousers and pushed them down with frantic hands. Once she had freed his manhood, she wrapped her hand around it, stroking and squeezing him.

"Slow down, my dear!" Knightley groaned. "Or I'll be gone before I'm even inside you."

"You're too slow, George. Always so slow," she panted. "I need it, fast."

"You always want it fast and rough." He unzipped the top part of her body suit and caressed her small breasts.

"Exasperating man!" She squirmed at his slow ministrations. Determined to hasten the speed of their love making, she cupped his balls and rubbed them roughly.

"Urgh!" he cried out. Grabbing her hands, he raised them wide to either side. "Slow down, Emma!" Then he lowered his mouth and licked her areola at a snail's pace.

Moaning, she held onto the gun shelves and arched her lower body outward to graze against him. But he moved his body an inch away, avoiding her glissade and keeping his own pace. His talented tongue swirled around the creamy flesh of her breasts, tasting every pore on her smooth skin. By the time he crouched down to kiss her navel, Emma had bitten her lips hard, her bottom rubbing back against the shelves.

Knightley eyed her face, which was twisted in a rapturous expression. Letting go of her wrists, he moved his hands down to remove her mini space skirt and G-string, still at a leisurely pace.

When the fabric grazed her sex, Emma gave a loud scream and reached her climax. Only when she was convulsing uncontrollably did Knightley picked her up, wrap her legs around his waist, and push into her with one slow and steady thrust.

"Oh my god, I'm going to come again," she cried out. Her hands abandoned the shelves and gripped his shoulders.

"No," he ordered, his voice low and savage. "Not so fast." He cradled her lean arse and ground against her unhurriedly, before withdrawing inch by inch, until he was barely within her entrance.

Her fingernails dug into his back as she tried to pull him back inside her aching warmth, but he ignored her frantic efforts and rubbed her folds with slow deliberation. He pushed again into her pulsing inner muscles.

Knightley's slow-motion love making was a torture for Emma, a euphoric torment that sent her muscles and every inch of her skin into sensory overload. She begged him for release twice more before he picked up his speed and pounded into her, again and again, finally allowing both of them to reach their orgasm with satisfying screams that echoed loudly off the walls of the armoury.

***

Inside a MIA warship, Commander Bill Collins brushed the two strands of hair on his forehead into place and straightened the lapels of his pink space suit. He was due for a conference with the Queen Immortal and wanted to look 110% impeccable.

"Commander Collins, Her Royal Highness will be on the air in 30 seconds."

"30 seconds! Is my makeup okay? How about my body suit? Mirror! Give me the mirror!" he yelled to his assistant, Alicia. When that didn't produce the mirror immediately, he ducked down and frantically searched the drawers of the table in front of him.

"Here's the mirror, sir. Hurry up! There is no time."

"I know, I know."

"Sir, 5, 4, 3, 2, 1."

"Where is Commander Collins?" the Queen cried out when she saw an empty conference room.

Collins stood up from under the table, hair dishevelled, sweat dripping down his forehead and leaving tracks through his mascara and foundation. "Immortal Queen of Earth, may Lord bless you with a thousand years of power," he gasped.

"I am extremely displeased. I am conducting the final training of the andudas, and I demanded not to be disturbed!"

"I'm terribly sorry to disturb Your Majesty's quality time with the adorable rats. But, your Majesty, a report of the most alarming nature reached my department, last night. It concerns your nephew, the esteemed Mr. Fitzwilliam Darcy. He was reported to have boarded Love Your Mate's capsule UR1 – as in *You Are the One* – disguised as a blond-haired man."

"Nonsense! Your source must be a hoax. Why would Darcy do such a thing? He can have any girl he wants at his residence for as long as he wants them, simply by punching a few keys on the keyboard. Why would he need to go out to one of those dirty hire-out places?"

"My Great Queen, you are right about those mating capsules being horrible establishments for immoral people…but I checked out my source with newly appointed Tea-Leaf Reader Wickham. He believes in the authenticity of the information, as well."

"How can that be?" she demanded frostily.

"My department conducts mass body index spy scans on all people entering mating capsules, then matches them with the national database. The honourable Mr. Fitzwilliam Darcy was on our alert list because of your directive that his sperm only be matched with Angelic Princess Anne de Bourgh. The spy scan alerted us, last night, that a man of near-identical mass body index as your nephew had entered UR1."

"Headstrong man! Darcy never listens to my instruction. Who was with him? And what have you done about it?"

"According to my investigation, the capsule seems to have been hired by a woman, half-Gentry, half-Merchant class, by the name of Eliza Bennet, using a pseudonym. We made a near-positive identification of her through the spy scan, as well. They met in Hertfordshire when he stayed at his friend Charles Bingley's new estate there. Eliza Bennet lives in the vicinity."

"Country, and a lowly chit! I would have thought Darcy to have better taste." She sighed heavily. "He is probably indulging in one of those one-night stands. I have heard that such capsules are well-equipped with condoms. Just let him be, and get rid of the woman later. I wouldn't want any bastard children showing up to trouble Anne in the future. And, when Darcy returns, I will give him a set down for patronising such an illegal establishments. It is not good for my public image."

"Absolutely, Majestic Queen! But I'm afraid the matter is a bit more complicated. This Eliza recently applied to the Reproduction Committee, wanting your nephew to father her child."

"What? How dare she?"

"Exactly! Wickham and I rejected her application and recommended that she reproduce with my sperm, instead, but she has taken the process no farther. If she invited Handsomest Mr. Fitzwilliam Darcy to the mating capsule, we suspect she either intends to use her arts and allurements to convince him to agree to her scheme…or she intends to kidnap him and steal his sperm."

"That cannot be borne! How dare she! What have you done about it? Where are they now?"

"I led a pursuit of the capsule as soon as the information seemed to point to your nephew being in danger; but the capsule had a head start on us. We did manage to shoot at them…"

"What! You shot them? But Darcy is in there! You wish to kill Anne's fiancé?"

"Indeed not, Your Majesty. I consulted Tea-Leaf Reader Wickham most carefully. We calculated this to be the best course of action. We did not want to shoot them down. We simply intended to frighten them into returning to Earth."

"Well then, where is he now?"

"The capsule was…umh…hit, unfortunately, and suffered a free fall. They have landed on Planet Hartfield."

The face of the Queen Immortal twisted red. She pondered for a minute before commenting. "The rebel planet? You have put my nephew and my throne in great danger. I will have your head on my table if Darcy is hurt! What if Hartfield used him as a bargaining chip?"

"Please don't be alarmed, my esteemed Queen. I consulted Wickham after the event. He said that it provided ample justification for the Queen to invade Planet Hartfield. He knows that it is a planet that your Majesty has long desired, because of its strategic location and resources, but had not yet found a legitimate reason for doing so."

The Queen paced around for another minute, thinking hard, and nodded. "Brilliant – as long as you and Wickham can guarantee Darcy's safety in the meantime."

"Wickham's tea leaves said so. We would not want to bring any harm to Ravishing Princess de Bourgh."

"Well, report back as soon as you have word. I need to go back to my pets."

"We will need Your Royal Highness to approve the number of warships we deploy, and the funding involved."

"I am scheduled to be in attendance at the andudas competition for the next two weeks. Ask Wickham to come to my chamber tonight. I want his personal reassurance as to Darcy's safety. I will give the seal to him then. You two can take care of things on your own, so long as you have my seal. I don't want to be disturbed during the next two weeks. Is that understood?"

Collins bowed low and replied, "Definitely, Queen Immortal. Enjoy your competition. We will send you good news once we seize Planet Hartfield and return with the esteemed Mr. Fitzwilliam Darcy."

"And remember, get rid of the country chit, or send her to one of the Gentry camps. That will teach her to have the audacity to want Darcy to father her children."

"Certainly, Immortal Queen of the Earth. May Lord bless you with a thousand years of prosperity."

***

Inside the mating capsule, Darcy tore his gaze away from the alluring bathing scene that Elizabeth presented. He was sorely tempted to join her, as his body was still greedy for her, but he set his mind to work, instead, and turned his attention to the crippled computer console. There would be time for love-making when they returned safely to Earth.

He hadn't wanted to fix the computer earlier, so soon after the soldiers left. Officer Woodhouse looked friendly and harmless, but Captain Knightley was another matter entirely. Darcy had seen him focus on the wigs on the floor, and had caught Knightley's slight frown when Elizabeth "forgot" to introduce him by his full name. Being a relative of the unpopular queen of Planet Earth had its benefits and its downsides. He was aware of his aunt's ambitions regarding Planet Hartfield, and he didn't want to be used by either side.

Aiming his ring towards the console, he activated a red beam to scan it. The answering tone that it generated identified the damaged area. Darcy flipped some tiny tools out from his ring and started the repair.

"So, you know how to fix a computer after all," she said.

Darcy turned to look at Elizabeth. Her mass of hair hung in a damp, tousled tangle down her back, but the wild appearance only made her appear more beautiful. Her cheeks were flushed a healthy pink and, although she wore the same body suit as before, she now smelled delightfully of lavender. He wanted more than anything to make love to her all night long, but time was of the essence. He simply nodded, then continued to work in silence for nearly half an hour.

Finally straightening from the task, he said, "I wanted to wait until the soldiers were well away, first. Now it's done. Do you want to check the software and see whether we can connect to galaxynet? Just be careful to use the backdoor."

"You're worried about Emma and Captain Knightley?"

"More about my aunt's ambition to invade Planet Hartfield."

"Is that so? Your aunt appears interested in so many other planets that I lose track."

"I heard her talking about it, some months ago. If she got wind of my being captured here, it would give her an excellent excuse to launch a military action. I don't want anyone hurt because of us."

Elizabeth agreed. "So I should avoid letting the host server know where or who we are."

"We don't know what people here might do, if they find out who I am."

"I know. I saw Knightley's reaction when I avoided using your full name. I will be careful in my communications."

Darcy's admiration for her increased another notch. She was smart and observant. "Try Netherfield or Pemberley," he advised, and added, "I'll take a quick shower and prepare some food while you try to make contact."

Elizabeth watched covertly as he walked past her and entered the bathroom, taking off his body suit in the process. She was mesmerised by the sight of his strong naked body for a minute before she realised the ramifications of the bathroom's transparency.

Blast the man! I bet he spied on me as I took my shower, just now.

As she blushed and cursed him under her breath, he turned and gave her a jaunty wave, revealing his powerful lower body to her gaze. Remembering her futile attempt in stealing his sperm earlier, Elizabeth's face grew even hotter. She immediately turned her attention back to the computer console. Finally after nearly a quarter of an hour, she managed to reach Bingley.

"Charles, we need your help."

"What has happened, Lizzy? Jane said you didn't return home, last night, and she was worried about…" His eyes widened. "Is that Darcy with you?"

She turned and found Darcy standing behind her, fully dressed.

"Charles, we were shot down by MIA. We've landed on Planet Hartfield. Can you contact Reynolds and organise a rescue?"

"I'm punching in the SOS code as we speak. I've gleaned your co-ordinates from the connection. Hang on a sec! Are you in one of the LYM capsules? The decor looks vaguely familiar."

Elizabeth was flustered at being found out. She began groping for words, hoping to invent some believable excuse, but Darcy simply sat down by her side. Wrapping his arm around her shoulders, he said to Bingley, "Should we tell Jane you're a frequent visitor of the mating capsules?"

"No! Lizzy, don't believe him. I have only been there a few times, back when I was very young."

"Yes, I'm sure that's what you would like us to believe. At any rate, Elizabeth and I spent the most spectacular night here. She has agreed to be my wife."

"You sly man! I didn't know you were pining after Lizzy. No wonder you've been so low in spirits, these past few months after we left Hertfordshire. Congratulations! Lizzy, my friend is the best, though he can be sometimes very annoying – such as on Sunday nights, when he has nothing to do. But I think he'll make you very happy. I will tell Jane now. Is there anything else you need me to tell Reynolds?"

"Just ask him to act quickly. He knows the delicacy of the situation here on Planet Hartfield."

"He surely does…" Suddenly the monitor went blank and Bingley dropped out of communication.

"What now?" Elizabeth typed in a few more commands, but the console was not responding.

"They might have blocked our communications."

"Damn! Do you think they know who you are?"

"Could be. Don't worry. My assistant Reynolds is very efficient."

Elizabeth nodded and stood up. "Whatever possessed you to tell Charles that we are going to get married?"

"Would you rather have him tell your sister that we simply lusted after each other and decided to hire a mating capsule? Or perhaps you wanted him to tell her that you just wanted to steal my sperm? Would that go over well with your family in Hertfordshire? I'm just trying to protect your reputation."

"It's the 39th Century! Women can do whatever they want."

"I'm an old-fashioned man. I don't want our child to be laughed at by others, saying that his or her mom is a heartless woman."

"I'm not heartless. I'm simply goal-oriented."

"Whatever you say. Come! Let's have a nap. We need to conserve energy, in case things take a turn for the worse, here. My head and shoulders still hurt." He stretched out on the bed and signalled for her to join him.

Elizabeth was annoyed with the man; he was so unpredictable. But before she could settle down on the makeshift bed on the floor instead of joining him, he forestalled her action.

"Could you possibly give my shoulders a rub? After all, I hurt them while protecting you."

Elizabeth hated to owe anyone a debt. She walked over, sat down by him, and began to massage him gently.

After several lulling minutes, he turned and tugged her gently down beside him. "Let me hold you," he entreated.

"I'd better go back to the bed on the floor," Elizabeth said.

"I'm not seducing you. I just want to hold you and rest. I'm tired. Aren't you?"

She lay rigidly beside him until she heard his breathing slow and deepen. Then, reassured, she drifted into sleep.

***

Back at the base, Emma and Knightley pursued their investigation into the identity of the male captive. After a wait of several minutes, they discovered that Darcy was one of the nephews of Queen Catherine on Earth.

"What should we do?" Emma asked, stunned.

"Two possibilities. One, he came here on a secret mission on behalf of the Queen. Two, he was a genuine LYM's patron."

"It took us less than ten minutes to verify his identity by comparing his body features to the underground galaxy database. I don't think he is acting as the Queen's spy."

"I don't think so, either."

"Should we simply treat him as a normal captive?"

"Definitely not! We can exchange him for some of our men who are imprisoned on Planet Earth. Let's go and bring Mr. Darcy and his woman back to the prisoner cell."

"That seems harsh. Perhaps we shouldn't alienate him? What if we take them into custody tomorrow, instead, when we bring them the supplies?" Emma suggested.

"Perhaps, after all, we don't work like the operatives of the Queen Immortal." Knightley considered the matter a moment longer. "It might be best if we simply go back now. We can explain our intentions to him."

"What if they resist our arrest? Should we request back-up?"

"No need. He's only an agriculturalist and Miss Bennet a programmer. I'm sure the two of us can handle them easily." With confident strides, Captain Knightley headed back to his cruiser.

Halfway to Darcy and Elizabeth's mating capsule, Knightley and Emma received an urgent command from Control. "Red alert! Red alert! An Earth warship has been detected at west 231876. Another unidentified vessel detected at east 127845. Captain Knightley to investigate the warship."

"Received, Control!" Knightley replied immediately, and turned the cruiser around towards the western coordinate.

Voting options

1) Darcy and Elizabeth escape from Captain Knightley's pursuit

2) Darcy and Elizabeth are locked up in the prison cell

3) Collins crashes his warship onto Planet Hartfield √

CHAPTER FIVE

Night had fallen on Earth. A handsome young man in a long, shoulder-to-floor purple robe made his way to the royal quarters of the Great Queen.

"Tea-Leaf-Reader Wickham to see the Queen Immortal!"

The maid led him to wait in the royal bedchamber. Not long after, Her Majesty made her entrance.

Wickham bowed low as she came in. "Your Majesty. May the Lord bless you with a thousand years of power!"

"Come, my dear." Queen Immortal put out her hands and gestured for Wickham to rise.

He straightened and gave the Queen a hug, then kissed her on the lips. "I've missed you, my darling!" Wickham told her with a grin.

"And I have missed you. Now tell me what you want," Queen Catherine said.

"I need your seal and approval for $9 million to take action against Planet Hartfield immediately."

"Darcy won't be hurt?"

"You know that my tea-leaves never fail. Didn't I predict your ascension to the throne? He won't be hurt. Indeed, he will become your son-in-law when the next full moon rises."

"Excellent. I shall give you the seal later on. For now, use your magic hands and give me a full-body massage," Queen Catherine directed as she disrobed and reclined on the bed.

Wickham bowed and did as he was told, smoothing scented oil over her body. Next, he sprinkled her skin with a magical herb powder that he had made himself, and worked hard on her shoulders, back, bottom and legs.

As he worked, he thought absently, *I spent over a year learning the skill of appeasing women, and it was all time well spent, for it has gotten me to this present status. I live as luxuriantly as Darcy, and have as many maids and servants to do my bidding. Life is good. Who cares if the women I work upon are old and wrinkled, with sagging breasts and foul-tasting folds?*

Wickham turned the Queen Immortal around and used his hands, mouth and tongue to pleasure her. After almost an hour, she smiled, drowsy and smug. "Ah, Wickham, you have worked wonders! What a pity that you no longer possess your family jewels, or you would be the most sought-after man on Earth," she murmured, and drifted off to sleep.

By her side, Wickham clenched his fists tight, holding the Royal seal with force, and vowed to destroy those who had reduced him to his present state. *My misfortune is heavy indeed!*

***

On board his command ship, which was cruising towards Hartfield, Commander Collins waited impatiently for backup. He hoped that Wickham's report to the Queen Immortal would be fruitful, and that it would result in at least three warships to help him attack the rebel planet.

"Commander, three cruisers from Hartfield are approaching us."

"What? I'm all alone here. I can't fight three! Contact Her Majesty immediately!" Collins replied.

His assistant, Alicia Boulanger, keyed in a few commands, listened intently, and informed him "The Queen is out of communication, for two weeks, sir."

"Two weeks?! Then put Tea-Leaf-Reader Wickham on! Should I turn back now, Alicia? What should I do?"

Alicia punched in a few more times and said, "Sorry, the tea-leaf-reader is not available, either."

"Oh my god, what should I do?"

"Commander, Captain Knightley aboard the Hartfield warship is requesting communication."

"What should I do?"

"Actually, the Captain looks quite handsome. I suppose there is no harm in talking to him."

Collins wiped the sweat from his forehead. "Oh, all right then. Put him on."

"Captain Knightley from Hartfield here. Your warship is approaching our border. Please state your business."

"Commander Collins here, on the business of the Queen Immortal of Planet Earth."

"And what might this business be?"

"We are looking for a man aboard an Earth cruiser. He may have gone past here, some time ago."

"Can you describe the cruiser or the man?"

"Umh, he's just an ordinary man from Planet Earth, and the cruiser belongs to one of Earth's private companies."

"He must be more than ordinary to incite the second-in-command on Earth to chase after him. Does he happen to be your Queen's nephew, Fitzwilliam Darcy?"

"Yes. Uh, no. Umh...yes. What have you done to him? If you hurt him, Hartfield will be in for a rough time. Our greatest and most esteemed Queen Immortal would send all her troops to destroy your planet in a second! Now, tell me where the great Fitzwilliam Darcy is."

Emma didn't like this greasy, stupid man, especially now that he had threatened her home. She retorted, "He is an intruder. We are permitted to interrogate him, according to galaxy law. He is in our maximum security prison, under Level 3 questioning protocol. We are interested in the real purpose behind his coming to our planet."

"What? Level 3 questioning is pure torture! Have you no wish to live? Alicia, cut the communication."

Alicia looked disappointed, as she was very interested in Captain Knightley. He looked more amiable than the Queen's nephew. It was a pity he had a prideful blond next to him. Repressing a sigh, Alicia did as the commander said.

"Now shoot them!"

"Are you sure, sir? They have three warships."

"Shoot them down! I will rescue the Queen's nephew myself! Mr. Darcy may not survive the torture, and you and I will be dead if the Queen should learn that her nephew was hurt and we did nothing about it."

Alicia shrugged her shoulders and locked the solar rays immediately to fire at the three Hartfield warships.

On the Hartfield ship, Captain Knightly shook his head. "Emma, you shouldn't give him a rise. Now see what you've done."

"But he threatened us first!" Emma protested.

Knightley shook his head again. He never could control his little sweetheart. She was too hot-headed for her own good.

"Alert! Alert!"

Knightley saw that their spaceship was being targeted by Commander Collins's spaceship.

"Sit tight!" Knightley yelled, and fired his torpedo against Collins, as did the other warships from Hartfield. He then instructed his colleagues to bring down Collins and his crew, but not to kill them. Hartfield was a peaceful planet. Knightley wanted to avoid fatalities and interplanetary incidents.

After several minutes of intense battle, the Earth warship was struck on the tail.

Alicia cried out, "Commander, we're hit. We're losing altitude. We'll crash soon!"

Collins held onto his chair, closed his eyes and waited for his fate. *I'm going to die. I'm going to die.* His whole body trembled, and he peed uncontrollably.

Bang! Bang!

A sudden loud noise and a great shattering shook the warship.

Collins opened his eyes and saw that his ship had crashed onto the ground. *I'm still alive!* He immediately unbuckled himself from the chair. Alicia and the rest of his crew appeared to be hurt, some bleeding, others moaning in pain. *They don't look like they have suffered any major injuries. I've no time for them.*

He opened the door of the warship and walked out. After adjusting his breathing apparatus, he took in his surroundings – a dense forest surrounded by a blue haze.

From the console in the arm of his spacesuit, he learned that he was on the wilderness side of Planet Hartfield. The gas was a strange mix of chemicals. It could be harmful to humans and could even make them hallucinate. Luckily, he was equipped with a breathing capsule.

Collins punched a few keys on the console and scanned for life forms. *Perhaps I can find the Queen's nephew, rescue him, and be awarded with the planet's highest order of bravery.* He pushed through the thick forest and advanced at a slow pace. *How I hate these spiky trees and ugly, gigantic flowers! Yuck, a pink reptile! And all this mud! I'm six inches deep in it, now. I really look almost wild.*

Collins walked for nearly three miles before the monitor on his console suddenly beeped, indicating that another life form was nearby. He slowed his steps, using the shrubs and trees to hide his whereabouts. *The life form is very near. But where is it?*

"We are here!" The mechanical voices of some creatures startled Collins. He turned around and saw three andudas looking at him with wide eyes. Although Collins referred them as 'giant rats' to the Queen, andudas were in fact descendents of cats and kangaroos, with huge heads, hopping bodies and strong tails. Straightening, Collins cleared this throat and addressed them.

"Bill Collins here. I'm looking for the maximum security prison on your planet."

"He looks cute, A2 and A3," one of the andudas said, and the other two nodded in unison. The machine-like sound of its voice was eerie in such a dark, intense environment. Collins took a deep breath. *I'm not afraid. Andudas are pets on Planet Earth. I'm much more intelligent than they are.*

"I like his two strands of hair, and the powder on his face. The eyes looked yucky though, A3 and A1," another of the andudas said. Once again, the other two nodded in unison.

"If you don't know where the maximum security prison is, then don't block my way, pets! I've important things to do!" Collins said, as he tried to ignore them and walk on.

"Pets? Do you think he's from Planet Earth, A1 and A2? Is he one of those bad people on Earth who make our brothers into pets?" the third anduda said, and the other two nodded together. Their countenances turned menacing, and they approached Collins slowly.

"Don't come near, you annoying, ugly pets, or I will shoot!" Collins pulled off his belt and raised it. It hardened into a spear, which he pointed at them.

"Let's tie him up, A2 and A3, and make *him* into a pet instead!" A1 hopped up at lightning speed. His strong tail swatted the weapon from Collins's hand, knocked Collins to the ground. A2 kicked Collins's arm over his head and sat on it. A3 then pulled a lengthy blue vine from his pouch and wound it around Collins's neck, torso and hands.

"Let go of me! Let go of me! I am the High Commander of Planet Earth! Our greatest and most esteemed Queen Immortal will send all her troops to destroy your planet, if you do not release me! She will make all of you disgusting andudas into pets. She will whip you and torture you and feed you poisonous fruit."

"His words are foul, A3 and A1," one of the andudas said, and knocked Collins's breathing apparatus off. Collins tried to hold his breath, but A2 stuffed something into his mouth. He finally let go of his breath and breathed in the blue gasses. Within seconds, his head felt fizzy, his eyes turned heavy, and he smiled, abandoning his struggles.

"You're our pet!" A3 said.

Collins nodded.

The three andudas climbed off of his body. A1 said, "Crawl on your hands and knees, and follow us."

Collins nodded affably again.

Happily, A1, A2 and A3 led the High Commander of Earth, in his pink body suit forward on all fours, secured by a vine leash as they made their way through the muddy forest towards the wilderness centre of Hartfield. Along the way, more and more andudas caught a glimpse of the strange man-pet.

Finally, they arrived at a giant entwined fig tree nearly ten meters tall. One of the andudas used its tail to press on a tree branch in a deliberate rhythm. After a few moments, a part of the tree base lifted up, and a pebble path appeared. The andudas jumped onto the pebble path, down the base of the tree and under the ground.

Collins crawled along behind them as obediently as a domestic pet. Down and around they went. The blue haze of the planet's surface atmosphere gradually dissipated. The High Commander felt as if his head was about to burst. He shook it a few times and gulped in deep breaths.

What am I doing? he thought. *Why am I crawling on the ground?* His thoughts were forming more clearly, and he realised that something had been stuffed into his mouth. Something was wrapped around his neck, and it was being used by someone to pull him along.

No! He was pulled by an animal – an anduda! He finally remembered his encounter with the vicious creatures. He wanted to stop crawling and demand that these damnable inferior animals release him. But his body felt shaky.

Looking around, he saw that he had been led into a cave-like space equipped with some shabby tables, chairs, cabinets and equipment, like a laboratory or factory. Several other andudas were busy nearby, but not jumping about, as andudas normally did. They, in fact, were walking awkwardly, and their hides were a range of skin colours other than brown.

"We've captured a bad man from Earth," one of Collins's captors said, and the others nodded. As the speaker released its hold on the leash, Collins gathered his strength, unwound the stinging vine from around his neck and struggled to stand.

"Where am I? Do you know who I am?" he demanded. "I am the High Commander from Planet Earth. I demand to be released and returned to my vessel immediately, or I will send a signal to my base, and they will dispatch warships to arrive at Hartfield within hours. My majestic and wise Queen Immortal will knock down every tree on this planet. She will round up all the andudas and lock you in our zoos, where you will be taught better manners."

A1, A2 and A3 looked at each other and then burst out laughing. The other hybrid andudas stopped their work and looked at Collins with wide eyes.

"Where did you find this piece of work?" a blue-skinned andudas by the cabinet asked.

"A3 saw his ship dropped, down by 829451."

"A2 saw him walking at 829892."

"A1 found him cute."

"I did not. Andubie, do not listen to him." A1 hopped closer to the blue andudas. "I thought this two-strand from Earth would be good for your experiment.

"Experiment?" Collins screeched. On hearing the intention of the andudas, he began to run back toward the passage they had come down. But before he could take more than a few steps, one of the walking andudas jumped in front of him and knocked him to the floor with its tail.

Collins yelled, "I am the High Commander of Earth! Stop this assault! My most respected Queen Immortal will launch an air strike on Hartfield if she hears about this."

"Put him on the table!" one of the hybrid andudas instructed. "He is not a good specimen but I do love to experiment on foul-mouthed humans."

Once the andudas had Collins secured on the table, they began making surgical incision on Collins's tissues, until the High Commander screamed himself unconscious.

***

Earlier, on Planet Hartfield, Darcy and Elizabeth had been awakened by the sound and light of the intense battle fire.

"Hartfield seems to be under attack," Darcy said as he looked out from the vision pocket.

"Do you think they'll discover your assistant's rescue ship?" Elizabeth asked.

"Let's go and check it out."

"But Captain Knightley said we were under surveillance."

"They are busy now. Maybe the surveillance won't be water-tight. Let's get some food and medical supplies."

Darcy gathered a few essentials into a bag and held out his hand.

Elizabeth looked at him and saw the confidence and determination in his face. She felt protected. She put her hand in his, and they walked out of the mating capsule together.

Once they were outside, Darcy manipulated his ring. "There. I've put a basic invisibility shield over us. Let see if we can fool Hartfield's surveillance. It's not the most advanced gadget in my ring, but it may suffice. Hmm, and I think Reynolds is coming from the east. Let's go and meet him."

"Your ring can tell that?"

"Easily. It's actually a mini-supercomputer with loads of gadgets. My sister, Georgiana, invented it when she was just thirteen. She likes to play with computers and invent things all day long," Darcy said with a proud smile.

"You love her."

"Yes, she's the best sister in the world."

Outside, the terrain was mountainous. There were hills and craters, with occasional vegetation, but barely any life forms. Fortunately, the air seemed to be normal, and they didn't need to use any breathing apparatus. They walked at a brisk pace and talked for about ten minutes, until they heard the sound of a cruiser approaching.

"Quick, let's find a shelter. We don't know if they are friends or enemies," Darcy warned, then took hold of Elizabeth's hand and moved in the direction of a small cliff dotted with sparse bushes.

But the cruiser appeared to have detected them, for it started to fire at them, not with fatal intent but as if it were trying to force them out in the open.

They ran up and down several hills, away from the laser fire.

"Damn!" Darcy yelled as he lost footing on the edge of one of the cliff face. He slipped and found himself dangling on the margin dangerously.

Elizabeth tried to hold onto him. "Hold on tight! Don't let go!" She cried out.

"I can't! Let go of me! I don't want to take you down, too." Darcy called out as he lost his grip on Elizabeth's hand.

"NO!" Elizabeth shouted as she saw Darcy falling down the crater. Without a second thought, she rolled over the edge and followed after him.

On and on they slid, farther down into the crater until they hit a big hole together – a long tunnel that seemed to lead them deep into the ground.

Darcy finally hit the end of the tunnel and dropped into freezing-cold water.

Splash!

Another splash brought Elizabeth down next to him.

He swam up to the surface. A moment later, Elizabeth emerged, too. "Elizabeth, are you hurt?" he called anxiously as he swam next to her.

She shook her head and hugged him tight. "And you? I thought I had lost you." She trembled, not knowing what had come over her.

Darcy returned her embrace. "No, I'll be with you, always," he promised, then kissed her with all of the pent-up fear and anxiety that the adventure of the past two days had awakened within him.

Clap! Clap! Clap!

"What a tender scene," a man's voice proclaimed, startling the lovers in the water.

Voting Options

1) The centre of Planet Hartfield is inhabited by a mad man

2) The man is instrumental in taking Darcy and Elizabeth out of Hartfield √

3 The man forces Darcy and Elizabeth to do some things √

CHAPTER SIX

Darcy and Elizabeth moved away from each other upon hearing the unexpected voice of a man. Turning, they discovered him standing by the edge of the lake. He was dressed in ancient clothing from Earth, possibly from as long ago as the 21st century. He looked to be in his late fifties, and was as tall as Darcy, but heavily built. His jacket and trousers looked to be of good quality, but they had been worn too long; they were torn and had holes here and there. He had curly, messy hair down to his hips, and his beard covered nearly all his face. He looked friendly, and yet there was a severe and intense gaze emanating from his eyes.

Elizabeth was the first to respond. She gave the man a friendly smile and said, in shortened breaths, "We lost our way and went over a cliff accidentally. That's how we ended up here. What is this place, sir?"

The man sat down on the ground, rested his elbows on his knees, and rested his chin in his right hand before replying, "This is the Heart. Young girl, you look gorgeous. Is that your hubby that you have been kissing madly?"

Elizabeth felt Darcy tense by her side, tightening his arm where it encircled her waist under the water. Elizabeth patted his shoulder, hoping he would relax. There was no use antagonizing the man. After all, he might tell them how to get out of the "heart." She said to the man, "Thank you, sir, for the compliment. My name is Elizabeth. This is my good friend Fitzwilliam. And you are?"

"Who am I? I don't know. I've been alone here for so long that I forget most things. Fitzwilliam and Elizabeth – I like the sound of that. Who are you to each other?"

Elizabeth's eyes widened and she turned to exchange a worried look with Darcy. "Are you saying that we are the first people you have seen for a long time?"

"People come and go. Who cares? Don't you want to come out of the water? Isn't it cold?"

"Yes, it's freezing." Elizabeth turned to look at Darcy, who nodded. They started to swim toward the shore slowly, all the while engaging the man in conversation. "People come and go? Then why didn't you go, too?"

"Why should I go?"

"Don't you have a family waiting for you?"

"Do I? I can't remember."

"How did you end up here?"

"Like you two, I suppose, dropping down from above." He pointed at the dark 'sky' which was the 'ground' of Planet Hartfield, "But I can't remember now. Some days, my memory is good and I can remember. Other days, it's so bad that I don't even remember the way here, and my head hurts as if there's a rock-hard molecule pounding it constantly."

"How many people have you met down here?"

"Who's counting?" he countered, and shrugged.

Elizabeth was getting increasingly frustrated with the man. She and Darcy had reached the shore near him, but when they emerged from the water, the man jumped up and backed away, shouting, "Who are you, young man? You look familiar."

"I'm Fitzwilliam. As Elizabeth told you, I'm her friend," Darcy replied.

"You look familiar…" the man repeated in agitation. Definitely familiar." He scratched his head, ruffled his hair and started pacing. "My head hurts! Why can't I remember?"

Seeing the man's unstable behaviour, Darcy took hold of Elizabeth's hand and tried to draw her away.

Suddenly, the man burst forward. He charged towards Darcy, knocked him to the ground and grabbed his throat with force. "You took her away from me! You seduced her! I'll kill you." He tightened his hold, strangling Darcy.

Elizabeth was quick to act. She jumped onto the mad man, thumping his back and grabbing his hands immediately. "Stop it!" When he didn't relax his hands, she shouted, "You don't know him. Fitzwilliam is not your rival. He didn't take her away."

The man relaxed his hold and turned to ask Elizabeth. "He didn't?"

Darcy took the opportunity to shove the man off his body. The stranger rolled away, but he dragged Elizabeth with him. Gripping her shoulders, showered kisses upon her cheeks, forehead and nose. "Sweetie! He didn't take you away. You're here. You're real!" His mouth was close to hers now. Elizabeth turned her head to one side to avoid him.

"He's mad!" Darcy shouted, and struck the man with a rock. The stranger collapsed heavily on top of Elizabeth, and Darcy pulled him away.

"He stinks too!" she added.

"Did he hurt you?"

"No," she assured him. "Did he hurt you?"

Darcy smoothed a hand over his throat and shook his head, as Elizabeth used her palm to rub away the unwanted evidence left behind by the strange man's wet kisses.

Elizabeth and Darcy hugged each other tightly for a moment, before checking on the man. He had been knocked unconscious by Darcy's blow, and there was a thin trail of blood on his head.

"I'd better take care of his wound. We don't want him to die." Elizabeth retrieved a few supplies from the wet bag Darcy still had on his back, and suited her actions to her words. Darcy had tried activating his ring but there was no signal from it.

When she had taken care of the man's injury, she asked, "What should we do next?"

"The temperature here is surprisingly hot. I thought, since the water was so cold, that the ground would be cold, too. Maybe we should leave him here while we explore this place. I don't think he'll come to any harm."

"Okay," Elizabeth agreed and then walked on, hand in hand.

The 'heart' of Hartfield seemed to be made of a lake. On the side where they had reached shore, the landscape was nearly barren, with rocks and no sign of life. As they walked on, more and more unknown trees and shrubs appeared. The ground became less flat, and some hills came into view at the northern end. When they finally reached the other side, they found a small cave with clothes and a jumble of belongings.

"It must be the man's shelter," Darcy said.

"Should we check out his possessions? They might offer some clue to his identity," Elizabeth suggested.

"Wouldn't that be an invasion of the gentleman's privacy?"

"Such a 'gentleman' that he nearly killed you!"

"He is just sick. I certainly wouldn't want people to go through my things," Darcy declared, and led her away.

Together, they walked on and found several more caves. At the farthest one, Darcy suggested that they spend the night, and Elizabeth agreed. When they had settled down, she said, "Take off your body suit."

Darcy tried to lighten the atmosphere. "You have the hots for me?"

She smacked his arm lightly. "I want to check on your shoulder and change the dressing. But I'll start with your head."

While she was ministering to his head, he pulled off the top of this body suit, baring his upper body. After she took care of the shoulder, they had some food from the bag he was still carrying.

"Such an adventure!" Elizabeth said, stretching out on the floor. "I definitely didn't expect to be shot down, captured and trapped in the centre of a planet when I invited you to the mating capsule."

Darcy settled beside her and gently brushed a few strands of hair away from her face. "I wouldn't want to trade this adventure for anything, and I certainly wouldn't want to share it with anyone but you," he murmured, gazed at her for a long minute, waiting for her to protest before leaning down to kiss her.

It was a slow and tender kiss. He wanted to take it slowly, but she returned it with enthusiasm. Sensing her response, he became more passionate. After a few minutes of hot kisses, they stopped to gasp for breath. Then he lowered his head again and suckled her earlobe.

Darcy felt her shiver as she ran her hands down his shoulders to his back. Now it was his turn to tremble. He unzipped her body suit and pushed his hands inside to caress her gorgeous, full breasts. They were bouncy and firm. When he squeezed her creamy mounds and plucked at her nipples, she dug her fingertips hard into his butt.

This set him on fire. He wanted to savour the moment, after their horrific day of life and death, but her eager responses overpowered his self-control. He surrendered to his animal instincts and quickly stripped her naked.

Elizabeth was not slow, either. She pushed the body suit off his lower body as fast as lightning.

Darcy lowered his head to suckle her breasts, while his hands parted her legs and worshipped her womanhood with his fingers, swiftly rendering her wet and hot. She moaned aloud, twisting and turning her body while venturing to grasp his shaft. Her untutored hands smoothed over his manhood with instinctive skill, alternately squeezing him and trailing a path over his hot skin.

Darcy panted heavily, unable to hold back any longer. He raised her legs, this time not just to his waist, but to his shoulders. He saw her eyes widen in concern over her vulnerability in such an exposed position. Gently, he said, "Trust me."

He pushed his thick and hard length into her, as slowly as he could manage.

Hot and forceful, at such an angle he seemed to invade every pore of her skin. She closed her eyes and arched her body. As he pushed deeper and deeper into her core, she felt sensations in muscles she had not known existed, and areas she could not bring herself to think of. It was as if two streams of hot lava had finally merged together to flow as one. She felt connected to him. They were one soul, and she responded with ardour, unable to resist.

Feeling her response, he pulled nearly out, then pounded into her again in a mighty thrust, no longer tender at all. He was maddened, like an animal possessed. He kept thrusting and thrusting, creating more friction against her inner muscles. He impaled her again and again, while his hands just as frantically kneaded and fondled her breasts.

She panted and moaned, more and more loudly. Her body was burning and sweating. Her hands scratched and rubbed his back and buttocks until she was tipped over the edge. She screamed and floated into heaven. Her whole body convulsed, squeezing him tightly.

He couldn't withstand her earth-shattering embrace, and reached his climax in the next second, trembling as he lost his control. His seed spilled into her, flooding her core.

He was spent, and collapsed on top of her.

Finally he found enough strength to roll off of her. He pulled her to his side, and they fell asleep in that tight embrace.

***

"Wake up, young man!"

Darcy opened his eyes and saw a laser sabre hovering over him. He saw that Elizabeth had been awakened by the man's words, as well. Luckily, they had pulled the body suits up to cover themselves as they slept, so they were not completely bared to the mad man's gaze, but the situation was not good. The stranger had a weapon, while Darcy had nothing except his ring.

"You don't look like my sweetie. You're not blond," the man said. "Come, young man. You have to start the learning. Otherwise, how can you take your love back to wherever you came from? Get dressed and come to my house now."

Then he left them and walked away.

"It must be a good day for him. He remembers, and he didn't kill us with his weapon," Elizabeth said.

Darcy gave her a quick kiss on the mouth and a tight hug. The full body contact sent shivers through both of them, but he moved away soon and started to dress. "What a pity we don't have time for a nice 'breakfast.'" He gazed at her tempting body. "But we had better do as he says. We don't want him to turn mad again."

She nodded shyly, still not used to waking up with this hot, nice Darcy. Dressing quickly, she went with him to do the mad man's bidding.

***

"You have to concentrate your mind on the rock, not on Elizabeth," the mad man said on a note of annoyance. He had been teaching Darcy psychokinesis for the past weeks. Yes, Darcy and Elizabeth had been trapped in the heart of Hartfield for nearly a month. The man had not had one relapse into madness in all that time.

Every day, he asked Darcy to eat some wild fruits. Glowing, they looked like dates and tasted quite sweet. He said they would help Darcy to acquire supernatural abilities. Then he would work at teaching Darcy telekinesis for hours on end. After the initial week, the man asked Elizabeth to take the fruit, and taught her, as well. They had to use their minds to lift things, to move objects and even to shape the laser sabre. With Elizabeth's company, Darcy was getting better and better every day. She also managed the skill with some success.

The young couple adjusted to living together, learning to trust, sharing their ideas, thoughts and worries. There was plenty of love-making and laughter, and a few tears.

At night, as had become their habit, they retired to their own cave.

On this night, two days and a month after their "arrival" at the Heart, Darcy was sitting with his back against the rock, toying with his ring. Suddenly, he pulled it off and threw it against the opposite wall. The sound of metal chipping the rock drew Elizabeth's attention away from her preparation of dinner.

"What's wrong?" She looked at his scowl with a frown. "Did you just throw away something?"

"It's nothing." His lips thinned, and he didn't raise his eyes to look at her.

She stopped her chore and walked to the end of the cave, searching through the leaves. When she saw the ring lying there, she crouched down to pick it up. She had seen it on his finger ever since they first met and, of course, she remembered how he had used it to free the magnetic handcuffs in the mating capsule, but she had never examined it closely before. It looked ordinary, like any ring for a man, although it was of exceptional quality and finish. She had never seen him taken it off before. Why now?

"Why did you throw it away?"

"Because it's useless! Georgie's invention is crap! I don't want to see it any more."

Elizabeth walked back and sat down besides Darcy. She tried to take his hand and slip the ring back onto his little finger but he snatched it away, jumped up and stalked to the entrance of the cave, looking out into the darkness of the "Heart."

"We've been here for weeks. The communication device in the ring has failed. There is no way up to Hartfield's surface. We'll be stuck here for months, or years. We could die here!"

"Surely not," Elizabeth murmured shakily as she rubbed the surface of the ring.

"We will! And what will happen to Georgiana when I don't return? She will be alone in the world!" he cried out in despair, and his hand struck the rock's surface sharply.

At the sound of the impact, Elizabeth jumped up. She pulled his hand down and examined it. There was no blood, but the skin was reddened. She let go of his hand and reached up to cradle his head. "Look at me, Fitzwilliam!"

He tried to turn his face away but she wouldn't let him.

"Look at me!"

He finally stared down at her, his brows knit together. He was biting his lip, breathing hard.

"Do you regret accepting my invitation?" She gazed at him, her fingers brushing his jaw.

"Never," he assured her. "But I have wondered...if it weren't for me being the Queen's nephew, would we have been brought down so soon?"

"You mustn't think like that. The MIA shoots at all mating capsules. I knew the risk when I invited you, and I'm sure you knew that, too." Upon seeing his nod, she continued. "We were shot down because of where we were, not because you're the Queen's relative."

His lips kissed her soothing fingers, and the scowl on his face eased, if only a tiny bit. He let out a loud sigh and murmured, "What if we are stuck here forever?"

She blinked her eyes. It wasn't that she had never thought of that possibility. But she was not a doom-and-gloom person, by nature. She had put that scenario out of her mind, with determination.

"I believe in fate, with a positive, cautious mind." She raised her head and touched his mouth again lightly. "I have always believed that we should make the best of every day. I'm happy that I share this time with you, rather than with any other man I have ever known. You make me feel protected and respected..."

He kissed her tenderly. "I love you, Elizabeth."

She nipped his lips. "You're the best of men, Fitzwilliam." With caring hands, she embraced him. Suddenly, she felt in her heart, after this long month of experiencing life with him, that he was truly an exceptional man. He undertook his duties diligently and he took prodigiously good care of those he loved. Elizabeth felt gratified to be loved by him. She cared about him, wanted him to be happy. She uttered the words to Darcy, without reservation, "And I love you, too."

His eyes glistened. "Will you put the ring back for me?" he murmured.

She took some cold water and washed his injured hand thoroughly before sliding the ring onto his little finger once again. "I will meet Georgiana," she said, and kissed the ring and his finger. "Soon!"

And, together, they retired for the night.

Darcy and Elizabeth also learned more about their strange companion, who referred to himself as 'Logan' or 'Laurie.' They settled on calling him Logan. He stated with confidence that he had a big house, a sweetie, a wife and a daughter, and that he was from Planet Earth. He still thought, from time to time, that Darcy was someone he knew. But, as he no longer confused Elizabeth with his sweetie, he didn't try to kill Darcy any more for seducing her.

They also learned that fewer than ten people had fallen down into the centre of Hartfield. Logan had managed to help each of them "out" after they fully mastered mind control and "communicated" with an electromagnetic disturbance that occurred from time to time. But where those people had gone, he had no clue.

As to why he didn't go with them, he replied that he had not felt such a rapport with those people as he did with Darcy and Elizabeth. And so, this time, he agreed that he would go with them, as well.

Logan explained how the mind control would work to take them back. "Every living organism is made of tiny particles. If you disintegrate an organism into tiny particles and regroup them later, you can send it through time and space. The same applies to your own body."

"So…if I was imagining the place I wanted to go, when the electromagnetic disturbance occurs, I would be sent there?" Elizabeth asked.

"I can't be absolutely certain, but that's the theory I have about the visitors who left the Heart." Logan replied

"But what if Fitzwilliam and I each pictured a different place?"

"Then I surmise that you and he would be sent back to different places – or even times."

As a result of that unsettling lesson, the young couple had agreed to concentrate on one place. As Longbourn was the only place they both knew well, they would think of it whenever they practiced the mind journey from Hartfield.

"And when will such an electromagnetic disturbance occur?" Elizabeth now asked.

"I don't have a clue, but they are not infrequent. Sometimes it's like an earthquake. Sometimes it's like non-stop lightning. I think it's due to something happening…up there."

"And what do you intend to picture in your mind?" she asked solicitously.

"I will think of the place where I last saw my sweetie."

"So we will end up in different places…" Right after Elizabeth's last word, a roaring sound began, and the ground they were standing on shook.

"This could be it!" Logan said "Let us hold hands together. Yes, I think the time is right."

Darcy and Elizabeth hugged each tightly, and pulled Logan into their embrace, rather than simply holding hands as he had suggested.

Logan murmured, "Perhaps we will all end up in one place, *my* place, as I have the strongest mind power."

Suddenly, the ground seemed to disappear – and so did their bodies, becoming weightless. To Darcy, it felt as if his whole body mass was dissolving into dust and bursting in the air. He seemed to have lost his hold on Elizabeth, and he panicked for a moment. But Logan's disembodied voice calmed him. "Concentrate on the place!" Darcy refocused and thought about Longbourn.

As quickly as the "disintegration" of his body had begun the journey, Darcy felt an explosive collision of every part of his body soon afterwards. He cried out in pain, aching everywhere for a seemingly endless time before he was finally able to open his eyes.

To his gratified astonishment, he saw that he was whole again, lying on lush green ground. He turned to look for Elizabeth and Logan, and breathed a sigh of relief when he saw both of them sprawled not far from him, apparently unharmed.

"Elizabeth, are you hurt?"

She moaned but replied, "No, although my body aches!"

"Mine, too. Logan?" Darcy asked.

The older man was groaning, but he had not yet opened his eyes.

"Where are we?" Elizabeth asked. "This is not Longbourn. The house is too grand."

Darcy turned to look, and said in a surprised tone, "Oh my god! It's Matlock!"

Voting Options

1) A murder occurs in Matlock

2) A revenge takes place in Matlock √

3) A separation happens in Matlock

CHAPTER SEVEN

"Matlock?" Elizabeth asked.

"The estate of my uncle, Lord Andrew Matlock. It's located some fifteen miles from Pemberley," Darcy replied.

"Were you thinking of it during the mind journey?" she added.

He shook his head in denial.

"Then it must be because of Logan. Could he be related to your uncle? Or..."

He continued, "...Or is my aunt, Lady Matlock, his sweetie? But my aunt is a modern woman...and Logan looks like he came from another century. He said we could transcend time if we mastered the mind skill. But I see no way of telling that from out here. Let's take him to the house."

They raised their aching bodies from the ground and went to help Logan up.

Not a minute into their walk towards the house, someone emerged from the wood and greeted them quietly. "Mr. Darcy! What a relief to find you," the man said in a low voice, casting an anxious glance over his shoulder. "Come with me at once. The General is waiting for you, and it's not safe to hang around here."

Darcy knew the man, who had been a trusted assistant to his cousin, General Richard Fitzwilliam, for many years. "Colonel Morgan, what're you doing here? Why is it not safe here?"

"Come. I'll take you to the General. He's in the mausoleum. Let me help you with this man." Morgan came to Elizabeth's side and relieved her, taking Logan's supported shoulder. He urged them to walk quickly and quietly into the wood, following the path to the family resting place.

"The mausoleum? Why is Richard there?" Darcy whispered.

"Things have changed drastically since you disappeared four weeks ago. The General will explain everything to you. I'm just glad you're finally back."

As they approached the mausoleum, Morgan threw three stones successively at one of the willow trees. Two armed guards emerged from hiding and came to meet them.

"Colonel," they greeted Morgan.

He nodded to them, then took Darcy and his party into the mausoleum.

A man in full military uniform who had been sitting in front of a computer atop one of the tombs, came down and walked to embrace Darcy.

"Darcy, it's really you! What a relief we have found you," the man said.

"Richard, what are you and your assistants doing here?" Darcy asked.

"My parents have been placed under house arrest, and I am wanted by the government," Richard replied.

"Whatever for?"

Before the general could answer, Elizabeth said, "Fitzwilliam, please put Logan down first. I want to check his vitals."

"Yes of course." They stretched Logan out on one of the invisible mattresses. While Elizabeth checked him over, Darcy said, "Richard, this is my wife, Elizabeth."

"You're married?" Richard asked, clearly surprised.

Darcy gave him a broad smile and a nod. "Yes. Elizabeth and I were married a week ago – in Hartfield," he said proudly, and thought back to that special day...

***

...Darcy woke from a deep sleep to find himself pillowed on Elizabeth's breasts – a happy circumstance that had become a habit of his, over the past weeks. He and she spent hours on lessons with Logan during the day. After that, they would walk hand in hand around the "Heart," talking about anything and everything. When they retired for the night, they would affirm their relationship with tender or fierce lovemaking. Sleep came to him easily, then, and he would normally wake up to find himself snuggled tightly against her.

But this time, before he could wake her with a kiss, Elizabeth stretched her hands above her head and awoke with a soft groan. Darcy loved the sight of her sleepy form. He traced his fingertips down from her neck to her supple bosom. The creamy mounds were silky to his touch.

She opened her eyes. "What do you think you're doing, sir?"

"I am waking up the lazy bone," he replied, and leaned down to suckle her nipple.

Elizabeth moaned aloud. His beard, which had been growing during the past weeks, tickled. She complained, "Who's the lazy one who doesn't shave?"

Darcy raised his head. "Who promised to be my slave, last night? Shouldn't you be earning your keep?" He rolled her toward him and gave her a playful slap her on the bottom. "Wake up and do your work!"

"Ouch! You were cheating, last night!" They had been playing striptease chess with stones, and Darcy bested her.

Elizabeth wrestled him around, straddled him and held his hands to his sides. "Now it's my turn!" She slapped him once on the thigh.

He did not feel any pain but raised his head to bite her nipple.

"Ouch!" Elizabeth yelled. Then her expression changed abruptly, and she scrambled off of his body, covered her mouth with her hands, and dashed out of the cave.

Seeing her strange behaviour, Darcy was alarmed. He rose and ran after her immediately. When he found her throwing up beside a tree, he asked anxiously, "Elizabeth, what has made you unwell?"

He saw her wipe her mouth with the back of her hand and shake her head. She looked very pale. He came near her and hugged her gently. "Elizabeth, please don't fall ill! You're my only reason for living, here in this hell hole." He choked out the words, and hugged her tighter, relieved when she returned his embrace. When he had himself under control, he looked at her.

She had tears in her eyes, but she wore a broad smile. "Fitzwilliam, I love you, too. And I'm not unwell. Truly. In fact, I'm very well. I think I'm pregnant."

He was stunned for a minute, his mouth gaping open. "I'm going to be a father?" He picked her up happily and swirled her around.

"Put me down, Fitzwilliam! You'll make me throw up again!" she warned.

He put her down immediately, and knelt before her. "Elizabeth, mother of my child, will you marry me?"

Elizabeth rolled her eyes and said with a pout, "So unromantic!"

"You can't blame me, my dearest and loveliest Elizabeth. This is my sixth proposal in the past weeks. It's only natural that my nerves and my words get worse and worse after each rejection." He pressed a hand to his heart and gave her an injured look.

She looked down at him and replied, "I will if you can catch me!" And with that she turned and ran back into the cave, where Darcy caught her easily on their 'bed.' He then worshipped her tenderly, not wanting to hurt the baby.

Not long after, as they recovered from their emotional lovemaking, they heard Logan's voice outside their cave. "Hey, in there! Time to work!"

Darcy raised his head from Elizabeth's breasts and said loudly, "We'll skip class today. We just got engaged!" He licked her nipples, making her moan aloud again.

"You want to get married?" Logan's asked in a surprised voice, much closer this time.

Groaning in frustration, Darcy turned and saw Logan walking into the cave. Immediately pulled several articles of clothing over to cover their bodies, Darcy said, "Can't you go away for a bit? It's not every day that I get engaged."

"I can marry you two now," Logan offered, and came to sit by them.

"Go away, Logan!"

"No. I want to marry you two now. You shouldn't wait. Life is uncertain. You never know what will happen next."

Elizabeth could hear a rising agitation in Logan's voice. She wondered if he was going to have a bad day. She certainly didn't want him to, so she asked, "How can we get married? We don't have a priest. We'll just have to wait till we return..." Her voice trailed off as she entertained the gloomy thought that they might never return to Earth, and that her children might never see a single day of sunlight.

"But I am a Lord," Logan insisted. "I have the authority to marry anyone in my estate. Come to my house, and I will marry the two of you. Darcy, you should have given Elizabeth your name long ago, seeing that you have taken her virtue." Then he stood up and walked away, looking stiff and uptight.

Darcy and Elizabeth looked at each other and decided to play along with him. They washed, got dressed and arrived at his cave, half an hour later.

To their surprise, Logan had his house all set up. There were candles and plants scattered here and there, making the stone cave look much like an altar in ancient times. He wore a long white robe that was quite clean over his normal clothes, and placed Elizabeth's and Darcy's hands on a religious book.

He conducted their wedding ceremony in an ancient Earth method. When Logan pronounced them husband and wife, and stated that Darcy might kiss his bride, Darcy first kissed her wrist, followed by a passionate yet tender kiss on the mouth. When the ceremony was finished, they felt truly married. Logan even gave them 'time off' from lessons and allowed them a day of 'honeymoon'...

***

"So, you really *were* stranded on Hartfield! I thought it was only an excuse for the government to invade the planet," Richard said, his voice startling Darcy out of his reverie.

Darcy stared at him. "Aunt Catherine has invaded Hartfield?"

"Let me explain everything," Richard said, and began the tale. Apparently the Queen Immortal had fallen ill during the weeks of andudas competition. She had entrusted the seal of the Planet to Tea-Leaf Reader Wickham, And he, in turn, sent several warships to attack Planet Hartfield because it was reported that Darcy was being held captive there and was being turned into a pet by the andudas on the planet. As Darcy was supposedly the future husband of Princess Anne, Earth would never allow such disrespectful treatment toward one of their most esteemed citizens.

"After a week of intense fighting, Wickham withdrew the troops and declared that you had been killed in the fighting. He also stated that, although Hartfield had not fallen, he had been successful in retrieving your 'body'. Then he claimed that his reading of the tea leaves indicated that Princess Anne should not go into mourning over your death. Rather, she should be married immediately, in order to bring joy to Earth and hopefully revive her mother's ailing health. Otherwise, the Queen Immortal would die. And so he married Anne, last week."

"What?! But he's not even a man!" Elizabeth blurted.

"What do you mean, he's not a man?" Darcy asked, confused.

Elizabeth replied, "Wickham stayed in Meryton for some time, and my youngest sister, Lydia, became deeply enamoured of him. She tried to seduce him, one night...only to discover that he is a eunuch."

Darcy and Richard looked at each other with wide eyes.

Facing Darcy directly, Elizabeth added, "He told Lydia that it was you who reduced him to his present state. That was why I've never consider asking him to father..."

"And you believed him?" Darcy asked in an affronted tone.

"Yes, I did, as did Lydia at the time, because you were so arrogant and conceited when we first met you. And I thought, 'Why would a man lie about such a horrific incident?' But, of course, I don't believe him any more – not after my clash with the Reproduction Committee, and especially now that I know you better!"

"But you never asked me about it when we were on Hartfield."

"We had more important things to talk about," she replied in a matter-of-fact tone, leaving him in no doubt that it had been some time since she had believed Wickham's tale.

Darcy's tense expression eased, and he nodded reluctantly before turning to Richard. "But how did Uncle and Aunt come to be under house arrest? And what about Georgiana?"

"Once Wickham became the Prince, he started arresting and persecuting the Noble class. He said a lot of them were in cahoots with Hartfield, conniving to bring about your death because they didn't want a member of the Gentry to become a royal if you were to marry Anne, and that the noblemen wanted to overthrow the Queen Immortal's rule. Almost all of us were placed under house arrest, executed or sent to camps, over these past days, for one excuse or another. Georgiana escaped before they raided Pemberley. Father and Mother are under house arrest. I am wanted and have been named in a warrant."

"Then why risk hiding here?"

"Truth to tell, the most dangerous place is often the safest. From here, I knew I could keep an eye on my parents and Pemberley, to see whether you or Georgiana had returned."

"Sorry to interrupt you," Elizabeth said, "but did Wickham or the government machine say anything about me disappearing with Fitzwilliam?"

Richard replied, "I'm sorry to pain you, but your whole family has been rounded up and sent to the dissident camps, except for Jane, who escaped with Bingley before the arrest. They said you were the lure used by noblemen to seduce Darcy into the mating capsule."

"Oh my goodness!" Elizabeth exclaimed, and crumpled to the ground.

Darcy went to her and wrapped his arm around her. "My dear, we will figure out how to free your family. Richard, what has been done, so far?"

Before Richard could answer, the ring on Darcy's hand beeped. Darcy looked at it and said, "It's Georgiana. She's near here, probably at Matlock House!"

"Damn! It's not safe there. Wickham has put out surveillance," Richard said anxiously. "I'll round up my men and we'll go in search of her."

***

Outside the house of Matlock, Georgiana walked as quietly as she could through the woods. She had finally received a signal from Darcy's ring, after so many nerve-wracking weeks of silence. She knew he was near.

But before she could enter the house through the secret passage in the woods, someone emerged and grabbed her. She screamed and kicked, but was quickly gagged. She was carried into the main house, where she found Wickham waiting in the grand ballroom.

"Well, well, what do we have here? My little Georgie." He signalled the men to tie her at a side table. Then he walked around her and said, in a menacing tone, "Bitch! I have been waiting for this for so long..." Taking out a knife, he placed the tip against her cheek, tracing it down her jaw, making a bloody line there.

"Revenge is sweet!"

Voting Options

1) Wickham takes Georgiana away from Matlock

2) Wickham escapes from Darcy and Richard

3) Princess Anne makes an appearance √

CHAPTER EIGHT

Wickham slowly traced the knife down Georgiana's neck, very close to her pulse. The bloody line got longer. Georgiana closed her eyes, determined to withstand the pain, but she couldn't prevent the tears that welled up.

He put the knife beside her head and removed her gag. Then he leaned closer, and yanked the zipper of her space suit down to her waist, baring her upper body.

Picking up the knife again, he continued to trace a line down her chest until the knife-point came to rest on the tip of her right nipple.

"So soft and innocent, my little Georgie. Shall I cut this beautiful nipple off, or shall I ask my men to worship it?"

Georgiana panted, her chest rising and falling more and more quickly as she listened to his threat. The knife-point thus made a deeper cut on her breast. Blood dripped out more quickly. She bit her teeth to fight the pain, and opened her eyes. Fashioning the most arrogant stare she could muster, she made her statement:

"Wickham cannot tell fortunes! He stole a defective prototype of a time machine image-projector that I invented to glimpse into the future. None of you should believe a word of what he says. Would a true messiah be so violent as to harm an unarmed girl like myself?"

Murmurs started in the room among the armed guards, but he laughed out loud then struck her on the cheek with a back-handed blow, knocking her almost unconscious and leaving a large red mark there, in addition to the bloody line.

"Don't believe this witch. Georgiana Darcy is a beast turned human who has to feed on man's essence to maintain her strength. Do you doubt it? Just look at what she did to me!" He slid open his red uniform, opened the fly of his trousers and displayed himself, showing the guards that he was no longer a whole man.

The gasps and murmurs became louder in the room.

"She bit off my manhood when she tried to seduce me, two years ago in Ramsgate. That was when I discovered that the Darcy family were all beasts-turned-human. Some of you have seen the body of her brother, which we brought back from Hartfield. Fitzwilliam Darcy showed his true form once he was dead – half anduda and half human. Now bring me some water."

One of the guards fetched the water for him immediately. Wickham splashed it onto Georgiana's face, fully waking her. He leaned down to breathe his next words on her face. "Now, does any one of you want to taste a beast woman?"

None of the guards came forward; they exchanged silent stares and fearful looks amongst themselves. They were afraid of what she might be able to do to them. On the other hand, they were also afraid of what Wickham would do. He was a bitter man with magic powers. Could he change their future if they did not comply?

"Don't be cowards. Do you want me to gag her again, so that she can't bite your ear off? But I'd rather not. I like to hear her scream. It's only fair justice for me to be able to hear her beg or cry out, in exchange for the pain and humiliation she has caused me." He tore her body suit farther open, baring her lower body, as well.

He continued to trace the knife down her abdomen, around her navel and down her apex. The bloody line was like a crack in the earth, contrasting with her porcelain-white skin.

Georgiana yelled in pain and raised her head to spit at him. "You're a disgrace, Wickham! I mourn for my father. He raised you like a son and granted you the privileges of the Gentry class. And what do you do with those advantages? You gamble, drink and trifle with innocent girls."

Wickham ignored her words, leaned down and bit her uninjured nipple hard, then used his fingers to grab a few strands of her pubic hair, which he cut off with the knife.

She continued, "All of you, listen! I didn't bite off his manhood. He drugged me and tried to rape me. But I hadn't consumed the whole drink, and I regained consciousness before he could do me harm. During our struggle, I accidentally activated the plasma knife in my watch, and it sliced his evil organ off. Did you know that I was not the first girl he forced himself upon? There are at least ten girls in Lambton that I know of who have suffered at his hand."

He raised his head and laughed out loud again. "Do you believe her?" The guards shook their head immediately. "A beast woman with a most persuasive tongue. Shall I cut it off so that she can no longer slander me? I, the esteemed husband of Princess Anne! I, who will be the King of Earth soon. I, who am so handsome – why would I have to drug and rape women? They fell at my feet, begging me to take them, when I was still a whole man. But I had high standards. I wouldn't sleep with just any woman. Some of them resented that, and slandered me instead. And you, little spoiled brat, you wanted me. When I wouldn't comply, out of my respect for your father, you laced my drink with a drug and bit my manhood off, whereupon that son-of-a-bitch brother of yours dumped me into the sea. It is only by God's will that I survived. I've been waiting for this day for far too long!"

He paced around the side table, touching his knife to her naked form from time to time when he became agitated during the speech. She cried out in pain, and almost lost consciousness again. Grabbing a handful of her blond hair, he cut it off. "I will reduce you to an ugly beast. You won't be a pretty woman after I'm done with you!"

He lowered his knife and poised it over her left nipple, using his other hand to pinch it hard. Before he could slide the knife across it, his hand froze.

"Bastard! Stop hurting my Sweetie!" Logan's voice thundered, loud and clear. He marched into the grand hall.

Wickham didn't know the man, and couldn't understand why his hands and legs couldn't move, but he knew that this man was not on his side. He ordered, "Kill the man! He's this witch's accomplice."

The guards moved to follow his order, preferring to deal with an old, dirty man rather than the young witch who could bite off a man's body parts. They jumped onto Logan but, with a wave of his hands, he conjured up a whirlwind and blew them all back. They felt themselves lifted off the ground, sliding across the ballroom floor until they were stacked against each other at the far end of the room in a heap.

Logan marched near the table, pushed the frozen Wickham off of Georgiana, and took off his robe to cover her. When she was freed, he untied her and hugged her close. "Sweetie, did that bastard hurt you? Don't worry. I will take you to Elizabeth. She has some medical equipment which can fix you up easily."

Georgiana didn't know the man, but she was thankful for his actions, and burst into tears. It had been horrible, running from the government's hound dog for the past weeks, not knowing where her brother was, or even whether he was still alive. Then, to discover a signal from him, only to be captured and tortured by Wickham, had been too much for her. She couldn't stop the tears.

"Shh, shh. Don't cry, Sweetie. All will be well. I'll take care of you." The man walked slowly toward the door, but before he could reach it, someone called out.

"Father, what have you done to my husband?"

Logan turned to see a sickly looking young woman in a sparkling tiara, wearing an elaborate court dress, crouching beside Wickham, who had been pushed by Logan onto the floor, trying to move his hands. The guards had all stood up, but they were plastered against the wall, not willing to come forward to confront the old man.

"This is your father? Sir Lewis? Why does he call Georgiana his Sweetie? Does she have a spell on him, too?" Wickham demanded.

"Anne?" Sir Lewis stopped. His eyes widened upon recognizing the woman beside the frozen man. He lowered Georgiana onto a chair nearby.

"You're Uncle Lewis?" Georgiana asked. She had never met him before, and he looked nothing like the portrait in Rosings, which had been her aunt Lady Catherine's home before she became the queen.

Sir Lewis turned to look at Georgiana. He scowled and repeated, "Uncle Lewis? You're not my Sweetie?"

"What's the name of your Sweetie, uncle?" she asked.

"You're not Anne?"

Georgiana shook her head, realizing that he was truly confused. "No, I am not Princess Anne. That is she.' She nodded her head in the direction of Anne and Wickham.

Sir Lewis shook his head. "No, I meant Lady Anne. You're not Lady Anne?"

"You mean… my mother?"

He looked incredulous. "Your mother? My Sweetie has a daughter? Are you my daughter?"

"I am the daughter of Lady Anne Fitzwilliam and George Darcy of Pemberley. I have a..."

Upon hearing those names, Sir Lewis looked angry. He smashed his fist onto the table next to where Georgiana sat, and yelled loudly, "That bloody George! He seduced my Sweetie! He took her away!"

"Father, please! Can you release George?" Princess Anne pled again.

"Why would I release George?" He turned to Princess Anne and continued his tirade of abuse. "He took Anne away, and left me with that bloody controlling, man-hating Catherine."

"No, I mean George Wickham, my husband here! Can you unfreeze him?"

"This worthless young man? Whyever did you marry him? He was torturing the young girl here. You're better off without him." He turned to Georgiana. "What's your name?"

"I'm Georgiana."

"Father, please!" Princess Anne called out.

"Oh, very well." With a flick of his hand, Sir Lewis released Wickham, who was suddenly able to move his limbs again.

"Where's your mother, young girl?" Sir Lewis asked Georgiana, as he continued his quest for his Sweetie.

"She passed away when I was three."

"What?!" He dropped down heavily next to her and then burst out crying.

Seeing that the old man was not a threat at the moment, Wickham hastily exited the ballroom from the other end, dragging an unwilling Princess Anne with him. The other guards followed suit.

Georgiana saw them leaving, but she couldn't do a thing to stop them, and she didn't know if it was a good idea to alert her uncle when he seemed so distraught over hearing about her mother's death.

As she tried to stop the bleeding on her chest, her watch beeped loudly. *Fitzwilliam must be near!* Then a group of men and a woman burst into the room.

"Georgie!" Darcy cried out upon seeing his sister sitting beside Logan. He ran to embrace her. "Logan, how did you get in here?"

When Sir Lewis raised his teary eyes, all he saw was a young George Darcy holding his Sweetie. Jumping up, he grabbed Darcy. "You killed Anne! Bloody George! I'm going to kill you!"

He knocked Darcy to the floor and pounced onto him, punching his face and stomach. Amid gasps and yells from the others, Richard was the first to act. He pulled the mad man from Darcy and restrained him.

"What are you doing, Logan? He's not George Wickham. He's Fitzwilliam Darcy!" Richard said.

Georgiana dragged her injured body to Darcy's side, arriving there just as Elizabeth did. "He's Uncle Lewis, Richard. Why did you call him Logan?" Georgiana demanded, recovering from the shock of her uncle attacking her brother. "He confused Fitzwilliam with Father. He doesn't seem to know that Mother died. He thinks Father took Mother away from him and killed her."

"Uncle Lewis?" Both Richard and Darcy were surprised.

Elizabeth had been smoothing her palms over Darcy's shoulders, to see if he was hurt. Now she turned and approached Sir Lewis, and said, "Logan, this is Darcy. He lived with you in the Heart for a few weeks, remember? You taught him your skill. He is not George Darcy. He did not seduce Lady Anne. Calm down please, and tell us what happened here."

Elizabeth's soft voice seemed to calm the struggling man, who replied, "I woke up and saw that you all had gone out. I didn't like the tombs, so I followed. I saw that you were all caught in the cross-fire with the army. I remembered Matlock well, so I went the other way to have a look. Then I saw a man, this George Wickham, torturing Georgiana, so I stopped him, but my daughter, Anne, came and asked me to release him. It seemed she's married to him, although I'd heard that this young woman here had bitten him off, and he was no longer a man. I'm all confused now. I have a headache. Elizabeth and Darcy, can we go back to the Heart? I don't like it here."

Elizabeth led him to a chair, sat him down and continued, "You have a rest. All will be fine, later on. But where are George Wickham and Princess Anne?"

"They probably left that way. Spineless man!" Sir Lewis said.

"Why did you dress in 21st-century clothes?" Elizabeth continued.

"I found them in one of the caves in the Heart. They are more comfortable than the space suit. What's the problem?"

Elizabeth shook her head and walked back to her husband's side.

"Georgie," Darcy said, "this is my wife, Elizabeth. Lizzy, she's Georgie."

Georgiana looked at Elizabeth with suspicion before turning back to her brother. "You're truly married to her? She was not simply a lure to trap you in the mating capsule?"

"No, Georgie. I love her. We love each other. We were married by Sir Lewis," Darcy said.

"Let me have a look at you. You're injured." Elizabeth said.

"We need to leave here and move to another safe location. Now that Wickham has left, and may know that Darcy is still alive, he may come back with more armed forces.

And, blast the man, he must have taken my parents with him, too," Richard said as he turned to pick up Georgiana.

Soon, the party retreated from Matlock and moved to a safe house in Lambton. Not long afterwards, major news broke out, shattering their short-term peace. It was imperative that they act at once!

∗∗∗

Thank you for tuning in for Prince Wickham's address to the nation.

The webcam panned to a handsome-looking Wickham, dressed in a fully decorated red regimental uniform. Since his marriage to Princess Anne, he had abandoned the Tea-Leaf Reader's plain robes for the more glamorous military uniform, as befitted a prince.

Sitting beside him was a pale-looking Princess Anne in her full white court dress. On a reclining couch was a motionless Queen Immortal. Wickham held Anne's hand, and said, in a charming and compassionate voice:

Our country men and women,

I am sorry to bring grievous news to you.

We have just learned that Princess Anne's former fiancé, Fitzwilliam Darcy, was not killed in the battle with Hartfield.

After careful DNA testing, we can confirm that the dead body we brought back from Hartfield was, in fact, that of our High Commander Billy Collins. He was captured by the andudas while serving the country's duty, trying to save Mr. Darcy.

Unfortunately, Commander Collins was tortured before his death, with his body experimentally fused with that of an anduda. We mourn the loss of a great man who died in the line of duty.

We have also received the alarming news that Mr. Darcy has returned to Earth, under mind control by the people of Hartfield, per the instruction of the rebellious Gentry.

He was seen with a vicious clone of Sir Lewis de Bourgh, my wife's dead father, and with his cousin, the fugitive ex-General Richard Fitzwilliam, his sister, Georgiana Darcy, and his whore, Elizabeth Bennet. Darcy's friend Charles Bingley and Elizabeth's eldest sister, Jane Bennet, are both still on the run, but have not been seen with them.

They are a dangerous group of people, and Sir Lewis's clone has been seen to perform harmful mind control against our soldiers.

In order to protect the good citizens on Earth, the government is willing to grant them leniency if they surrender themselves.

We will give them 10 days, until the 26th of November, to give themselves up. If they do not, the government will have no choice but to execute the following people now in dissident camps in London for aiding and abetting the rebels. They are family members of the fugitives, including former Lord and Lady Matlock, Thomas Bennet, Fanny Bennet, Mary and Catherine Bennet.

Our dear countrymen and women, you are urged to provide information about this dangerous group of people. We will reward those who come forward with useful clues as to their whereabouts.

You are also encouraged to attend the execution, should this be required, to witness the end of an era for the bad elements on Earth.

In this difficult time of struggle, we must be strong for each other.

As you can see, our Queen is still gravely ill. We have spent tremendous manpower and resources in the battle with

Hartfield. We hope you will give generous emotional and material support to the army.

After we remove this bad element, our planet will be cleansed, and life will be happy and peaceful again. May the Lord bless you all!

Voting Options

1) *Richard and Sir Lewis surrender to the government*

2) *Darcy and Elizabeth's baby creates havocs*

3) Bingley's reappearance thickens the plot √

CHAPTER NINE

Five more days!

It was the twenty-first of November.

For the past five days, Darcy and the rest of the men had disguised themselves and gone out, when day broke, to sway people's opinion and prepare for the rescue of the captives. Elizabeth, Georgiana and Sir Lewis stayed in the safe house in Lambton, where Elizabeth took care of the two patients. The three of them worked on the computer together, as well, monitoring news and helping to make sure that Sir Lewis didn't have a 'bad day' attack.

Today, Darcy returned to the safe house late. After dinner, Elizabeth had a towel ready for him when he came out of the shower. But instead of drying himself, he stood naked in front of her, water dripping from his hair and chest, while he looked at her intently.

Then he raised his hands to take off her nightgown.

"You're beautiful!" he whispered, and gave her a tender kiss. When her hands began to wander over his body, caressing his muscular torso and angular back, he shivered at the surge of arousal that swept through him.

Deepening their kiss, he pressed her body against the door. The droplets of water on his body made her wet, as well. He licked her lush breasts, which had become even fuller due to her pregnancy. He lowered himself and worshiped her slightly protruded belly. He loved kissing her soft, velvety body, and he grew more and more excited.

When he knelt before her and moved to kiss her apex, she grabbed his hair and uttered breathlessly, "Come inside me!"

Eagerly, he stood up and hoisted her up to his body. "It's not too rough for you like this?" he asked with concern, "Should we continue on the bed?"

She shook her head frantically and wrapped her legs around his waist.

He didn't need any further encouragement. Rubbing her folds, he slid a finger into her warmth, and found her wet and ready. He pleasured her for several minutes, teasing and stroking until he made her squirm and moan. Then he slid his finger out and positioned himself, pushing into her slowly.

Since learning of her pregnancy, he had tried to curb his ardour by going more slowly, as he was doing now. He sank into her inch by inch until he was at the hilt, enjoying her welcoming tightness and heat. Their souls were connected. They were but one person.

Soon, he started thrusting. In slow waves of motion, he moved in and out of her, creating tingling friction against her inner muscles that infiltrated deep into her bones.

He continued to kiss her luscious lips and caressed her sensitive nipples, enjoying the luxury of devouring her dreamily. After endless minutes of pleasure, her moans grew louder, quickening until she screamed out in satisfaction. Her inner muscles squeezed his shaft again and again, sending him into a vortex of climax, as well.

When they had regained their strength, they took a quick shower. Afterward, he lay on the bed, and she rested her head on his shoulder, rousing herself to ask, "How did it go today?"

"I went with Colonel Morgan to Rushcliffe, while the others tackled Charnwood, Bolton, Kirklees and other towns. The tide seems to be turning in our favour."

"You think so?"

"Yes. In most of the forbidden forums where we participate, people were questioning Wickham's speech and actions."

"May I read them?" she asked.

He lifted the X-pod from the side table and activated the screen.

Lara: Our Prince is as handsome as ever

Saxon: Yuck! He's a two-headed snake!

Moron: Lower your voice or yul b arrested 4 bashing the gov

Saxon: Im so shaking!

Idiot: Hes no brainer. Last speech said the Wax face* wld recover if he got hitched with Sickly but Wax stil looks like shit

Greatleg: He wont spare the captives, even if Darcy surrenders

Powerfinger: Course not. He said different things at different times. No trusting him

Wiseman: LOL. Last time he blamed the nobles, now its gentry. No pleasing him.

Lovelace: Still, hes charming. Pity Sickly's around.

---

* *Wax face = Queen Immortal, Sickly = Princess Anne, Brunette = Elizabeth, Hunk = Darcy, 2 hair = Collins, Tea-leaf = Prince Wickham*

Crush: Darcy's hunkier. Pity hes shagging brunette.

Bigchest: I know the Bennets. They know no Hartfields. Lydia may part her legs for any man, but not Lizzy and Jane.

Moron: HUSH or yul be arrested for aiding and abetting the rebs

Tower: I know Matlock and general - pretty easy going. No foreign pleasers

Moron: Now yul be arrested for fraternizing with nobles

Idiot: And what can be stupider? Confusing 2 hair with hunk. 2 hair's at least a foot shorter than hunk.

Wiseman: Maybe andudas on Hartfield made 2 hair taller during experiment

Stunning: I pity the anduda who fused with 2 hair. Hes gross.

Checker: Clone? Why would anyone want to clone Wax-face's hubby? Do they have no compassion for the man?

Saxon: Women! No wonder Earth's a mess. We've been ruled by the weaker sex for too long.

Crush: BS. With Tea-Leaf, we are even worse!

Idiot: Agreed. He wants money and men for his own

Crush: I hear hes building a huge spaceship called Ramsgate.

Saxon: 4 escape?

Moron: (in whisper) RA planning attack b4 execution.

Lara: RA?

Lovelace: *rolls eyes* even I know. Resistance Alliance!

Lara: Uh-oh, revolution? Shud I pack and go 2 Hartfield? The new Genl Knightley's yummy.

Idiot: Women!

Crush: (in whisper) Whos heading RA? how r they planning assault?

Wiseman: Let's talk on another channel.

"It's encouraging to know that people are questioning Wickham." Elizabeth said.

"And Richard reports that the number of people joining the RA has quadrupled since Wickham's televised speech. We should be set to storm the prison before the twenty-sixth of November."

"So we will set off the on twenty-fourth, as discussed. Do you still think Georgie and Sir Lewis are up to it?"

"I think so. Georgie told me that her electromagnetic treatment on Uncle Lewis seemed to be working well. His headache was less severe, and he seems to remember more and more about the early years of his life. She has been developing a special helmet for him that can be activated to calm him with treatment shocks when one of his strange moods overtakes him. I think his mind-control skill will come in handy when we rescue the captives. And Georgie can protect you when I'm in action. Richard's assistant has been training her on self-defence techniques and the use of weapons."

"Yep, Colonel Regan taught me, too," Elizabeth said.

Darcy frowned. "I told you not to overdo. I hope you haven't tired yourself."

"I'm fine. I don't have morning sickness anymore. In fact, I feel very fit. I..." She stopped suddenly, and her mouth gaped open.

"What's it?" Darcy asked, fighting down panic.

But Elizabeth was smiling. "The baby moved!" she said excitedly, and pressed a hand to her belly. Then her smile faded. "But how can that be? I'm only six weeks along. I thought babies didn't move until the twelfth week."

"Lie down," Darcy urged. "I'll check you out with the mediscan." He hurried out to fetch it but, when he returned to the bed, he nearly dropped the scanner. "Elizabeth," he exclaimed, "your belly's glowing!"

She raised her head and looked down at herself. "Oh my god!" She pressed her hands to her abdomen. "It doesn't feel strange... but..." Her mouth opened wider and she began to pant.

"What's it?" Darcy asked, and put his hand on her belly as well. "Oh my god!"

He could feel the baby moving. It was the strangest sensation, as if the baby wanted to respond to his touch but only had the weakest of energy. Still, their hands seemed to touch, for the slightest moment. Even more shockingly, he found that he could 'hear' the baby talk – definitely the sound of a tiny male voice: *Hello, Daddy and Mommy.*

Darcy and Elizabeth dropped their hands, in unison, and Elizabeth gasped, "How can that be possible?"

"You heard him say hello, too?" Darcy asked, pointing at her glowing belly.

Elizabeth nodded. "Use the mediscan." she said weakly, and breathed deeply to calm herself.

Darcy pressed the necessary buttons and scanned her body from head to toe, holding the machine with trembling hands. Then, together, they looked at the result.

"Everything seems normal. His body size and development are normal for a six-week-old baby. But... Hang on. Look at this!" Darcy swallowed and continued. "His brain is too well developed! The neurons are almost as developed as those of a three-year-old child."

They looked at each other incredulously. Three years old!

"Oh, Fitzwilliam, what can we do? What will happen to him? Will he born safely if his brain continues to develop so quickly!"

"I don't know," he was forced to admit, and wrapped his hands around her shoulders. Their bodies touched, and he heard the baby's voice again: *Don't worry. I'll be fine.*

Darcy moved away from her immediately.

"He knows we're worried," Elizabeth said in astonishment. "Do you think he knows why he can talk, too?"

"I'm not sure. But let's 'talk' to him," Darcy said. He pulled her hand and they put their hands on her belly again.

"Hello, son," he said slowly.

Hello again, Mom and Dad, the baby said.

"You can hear, talk and think?" he asked, "But it's too early for a baby to be able to do those things. Do you know why this is happening?"

But, Dad, I'm not a baby! My brain is quite well developed, much better than a three-year-old's, he replied with a confident arrogance that reminded his mother of the Darcy she had first met in Meryton. *And of course I know why this is happening. It was the glowing dates that the two of you ate, in the Heart. They stimulated my brain development. That's also why the two of you can do some mind-control, though you are bad at it.*

Darcy swallowed hard and asked, "So, what more can you do?"

Other parts of my body are still like a baby, unfortunately. I've been able to hear and think for a while, but I've only just begun to be able to talk. Today is great. I can move my legs and arms slightly, too. That was why I gave you a kick. But I think I can mind-control much better than you two.

His parents exclaimed, "What? You can mind-control?"

Of course. Today, when mommy was visiting Uncle Lewis, he talked to me through the mind and taught me how to do mind-control. It was hard, at first. He taught me to pinch Auntie Georgie's leg and it worked. And he explained to me that my brain might have been affected by the dates.

"Oh, so that was you!" Elizabeth said. She turned to Darcy and said, "I was chatting with Georgie at the time. She was adjusting the dosage of shocks on Uncle Lewis's electromagnetic helmet when she suddenly felt a pinch and yelped. We both thought it was a mosquito or something. No wonder I saw your uncle wearing a smug expression afterwards. He's teaching our son mischief!"

"Shit!" Darcy swore.

"Fitzwilliam, mind your language in front of the baby."

Mom, I told you, I'm not a baby! Not really. I've heard all the swearing by Uncle Richard, Morgan and the others for days.

"Damn!" This time, it was Elizabeth who swore.

Darcy smoothed his hand down her arm and said, "We need to decide on a name for him. We can't just call him 'Baby' anymore."

Uncle called me Logan, the baby said. *He said he liked the name. It reminded him of the happiest times he had with you two in Hartfield. Since he can't use it now, he wants me to have it, and that's fine with me.*

Darcy and Elizabeth looked at each other and rolled their eyes, but they were genuinely fond of the old man, too, so they nodded their agreement.

"But are you sure that your body is fine, Logan?" Elizabeth asked anxiously.

Don't be a worrier. You'll age quickly if you frown so much. I eat well and I learn heaps when you surf the galaxynet. It's cool that Auntie Georgie's computer talks. Logan added, *Oh, and I sleep well, too, especially when Dad makes love to you. The rocking motion seems to send me right to sleep.*

"Shit!" "Damn!" His parents swore in unison.

It's fine, Logan assured them, and giggled, *I don't see anything. Anyway, I'm sleepy now. Night-night!*

"Shit!" "Damn!" Darcy and Elizabeth swore again, not daring to touch each other. Then they broke into wry chuckles. "My goodness!" Elizabeth said. "No more love-making until the naughty boy is born."

"But that's months away! It's so unfair," he complained, and frowned. "Do you think he'll really be fine when he's born?"

She tiptoed to give him a peck on the lips, and said, "Let's not worry now. I will check up on his development every day. For now, we have to concentrate on getting our family out."

He nodded and wrapped his arms around her. Soon afterward, they retired for the night and drifted off into a peaceful sleep.

The next morning, they were awakened by the others. Dressing quickly, they went out to meet everyone.

"What is it, Richard?" Darcy asked.

His cousin waved his hand, and the computer screen moved towards them. His face was grim, his lips pressed into a thin line.

"Breaking news from Political Reality. Prince Wickham is happy to announce that rebels Jane Bennet and Charles Bingley were turned over to the authorities by the latter's sister, Caroline Bingley."

The camera panned to show Jane and Bingley, both of whom seemed to have been drugged. They were leaning on two armed guards, and their wrists and ankles were handcuffed.

Elizabeth gasped, and her husband wrapped his arms around her. Tears welled in her eyes as they continued to watch.

On the monitor, Caroline was visible, dressed in a shiny orange bodysuit that looked brand-new. She wore heavy make-up, and her hair was crafted into a big tower. She was smiling as she shook Wickham's hand warmly.

"Prince Wickham, C Denny from Political Reality. Your appeal works wonders. Even Charles Bingley's family has turned against him."

"Yes, I commend Miss Bingley's brave action." Wickham said with charming voice, *"She's honest and loyal to the government, and deserves to be rewarded."*

"What's your plan for these latest two fugitives, Your Majesty?"

"We will interrogate them to ascertain whether they know the whereabouts of any of the other rebels. If Mr. Bingley is cooperative and provides us with valuable intelligence, he will be spared from execution, due to his connection with the courageous Miss Bingley here." He nodded to Caroline and continued, *"But we cannot spare this fallen woman, Jane Bennet. She will be locked up with the other Bennets and treated the same."*

Wickham then left, and the interview continued.

"Miss Bingley, was it difficult for you to surrender your loved one?"

"Definitely not! My first loyalty is always to the government. Although I believe my brother was innocent of the charges, I still think it was best to deliver him into the hands of the authorities."

"Why do you think he's innocent?"

"Charles is very easily influenced by others," she said with a shaky voice, and pulled out a handkerchief to dab at her

teary eyes, *"I suspect the rebels used this whore to make him lose all sense of right and wrong. He's such a loving person, I can't believe he would actively work with rebels."*

"And what happened today?"

"He turned up at my place. He said they were tired of running. I could see regret in his eyes. I'm sure it was regret for associating with such a woman." Caroline turned to point at Jane, then added angrily, *"This woman was clinging to him like poison ivy, unwilling to forgo its prey. So I gave them some wine with a drug laced in it, and brought them here."*

"And you're fine with Prince Wickham's decision about your brother?" Reporter Denny asked.

"Of course, the wise Prince Wickham!" Caroline cooed. *"When the authorities talk to Charles separately from the vile woman, I'm sure he'll see what he has done wrong, and tell them where the fugitives are. I am happy for Prince Wickham's leniency."*

"What about the reward? What do you want?"

Caroline batted her eyes and said, *"I wasn't thinking of the reward when I decided to surrender Charles. It's for the good of the empire. But if the Prince still insists, I will be happy for a chance to serve under him."*

"Turn it off! I'm sick of the woman!" Darcy said angrily.

"Jane!" Elizabeth cried out, and wept, while he embraced her tightly and tried to calm her.

"Elizabeth, we will save your family!" everyone in the room vowed.

Voting Options

1) General Knightley visits the Earth

2) Sir Lewis comes face to face with his wife √

3) Charles is not what he seems

CHAPTER TEN

24th of November

At the Tower of London, Mrs. Bennet and two of her daughters, Mary and Kitty, had been locked in a cell together for many weeks. Three days earlier, her eldest daughter, Jane, had been brought in, as well. The middle-aged lady had been all nerves and hysteria; she did not even know why they had been arrested. No one had told her anything. She had not seen Elizabeth, Lydia or her husband for some time.

Jane brought them distressing news about Charles and their run from the authorities, and about Wickham's broadcast. Mrs. Bennet had been crying non-stop since then. This evening, however, Jane had told her some news that lifted her spirits.

"So, we are going to break out soon?" Mrs. Bennet whispered.

"Yes, Charles has been coordinating with the RA."

"The what?"

"The Resistance Alliance. We will start our action in fifteen minutes," Jane said in a low voice as she took a glance at the clock outside of their cell.

"But how?"

"Charles says that he is not what he seems. Their family has a special implanted ability. He has never used it before, but he will do so now, to help us."

"What kind of talent?" Kitty asked.

"He said we would see for ourselves," Jane replied. "I'm a bit worried about him, though. He did not seem to want to use this mysterious ability, whatever it is. I hope it won't be harmful to him."

"Is that why he asked Caroline to turn the two of you over to the authorities?" Mary asked.

"Caroline doesn't know of our plan." Jane shook her head. "Someone from the RA suggested that Charles try her. They believed she was pro-royalty and might turn us in. It was easier and more convincing than initiating a capture by the authorities."

"That's horrible!" Kitty said. "She really drugged Charles and you?"

"We were prepared. We took some an antidote that enabled us to keep our wits about us, and we assessed how things went. If we had not been brought in here with you, we would have broken out again. I expect that Charles is locked up with Papa right now."

"But what is the plan?" Mrs. Bennet asked anxiously. "Do we simply wait for Charles to rescue us?"

"No. If there is a male guard," Jane said with a blush, "I need to seduce him, at 0900 hours."

"But you're so shy, Jane! I don't think you'll capable of doing that very well," Mary said sceptically. "How about you, Kitty? I have seen you and Lydia flirt with many officers in Meryton, in happier times. And you are prettier than I."

Cough! Cough! "I can try," Kitty said in a trembling voice. "Jane, what do you want me to do?"

"They said that I — I mean you — should pretend to have food poisoning." Jane was happy to give up the seduction duty, and she hastened to explain the plan to Kitty. "You squirm on the ground, preferably with your dress parted, so that when the guard comes in, he'll see a bit of your chest. Ask him to take you out for treatment, and when you're all over him, we will overtake him. Charles will break out at 0906.30. That will give us six and a half minutes. The RA will be storming the building from the outside, at that same time."

"How will they know where we are locked up?" Mary asked.

"Charles implanted a tiny tracker in his left little toe," Jane said, "so the RA knows our exact location."

"But how can we do that?" Mrs. Bennet dithered. "I mean, how can we overtake the guard? We have no weapons."

Jane slipped her hands under her clothes and removed her bra. She manipulated the underwire a few times, to reveal a tiny needle there.

"Here's our weapon." Jane said, "Kitty, scream."

Kitty opened her mouth, but no sound came out.

"Come on, Kitty!" Mary urged. "You can do it."

Kitty shook her head and grabbed the neck of her dress tightly together, instead of parting it.

"I'll do it," Mrs. Bennet said impatiently. She unbuttoned her bodice quickly and lay down on the floor with her back to the cell door, then screamed at the top of her voice.

"Mother!"

"Mama!"

"Mom!"

None of her daughters were prepared for her quick action. They cried out in genuine concern.

The guard looked in and said, "What the heck?"

"It's Mom," Kitty said tearfully. "She's... she's not... feeling well."

Mrs. Bennet moaned loudly. "My stomach! My nerves! I'm dying!"

"Shut up, you old cow!" the man yelled.

But Mrs. Bennet took that moment to turn her body. Her hands covered her stomach, but her bra was askew, revealing a glimpse of her big breasts.

She peeked at the guard from under her eye lashes. *Good! It's the old goat.* The man was in his late fifties. She could see that his eyes had widened.

"What're you doing?" the man demanded. "Why did you open up your shirt? Are you trying to seduce me?"

Mrs. Bennet squirmed and shook. Her daughters' mouths gaped opened; they were too surprised to utter a word. She gripped her stomach more desperately and cried out tearfully, "My body is on fire! What did you put in the lamb? Why on Earth would I want to seduce you? My husband is ten times the man that you are."

Her taunting words hit the man hard. "I'll show you who's better!" He unlocked the cell door and strode in.

As he crouched down by Mrs. Bennet's side, Jane took a quick look outside. The corridor was eerily silent. No other guard was around.

She didn't know where Charles was, but she acted accordingly. Jumping onto the unsuspecting man's back, she punched the needle hard into his neck.

He reared up immediately, and pushed her off angrily, then prepared to follow up with a kick at Jane, but Mrs. Bennet grabbed Jane's bra, slung it around his neck from behind, and pulled it tight.

He was caught off guard, and began to choke. When he tried to turn his body to strike out at Mrs. Bennet, Mary kicked him where it would hurt him the most. He doubled over and then lay flat, face down. His glare was furious, but he seemed unable to raise his hands or body.

"Did I kill him?" Mrs. Bennet asked breathlessly.

"No," Jane replied, "it's the needle. It took a minute for it to take effect. It was coated with a special chemical and, when it reacted with his blood, it made him lose his strength. Now hurry! Let's go!" She hurried her sisters and mother out of the room and locked the guard in.

"Which way?" Mary asked, looking to the left and the right in the corridor.

Jane bit her lip. "I've no clue. When they brought me in, they twisted and turned so many times, I lost track."

As they stood there, undecided, a loud noise reverberated in the distance on their left.

"Should we go and check it out?" Kitty asked.

"Heavens, no!" Mrs. Bennet buttoned her bodice, reverting to her nervous self. After the incident inside the cell, all her courage seemed to be gone. "It may be the guards fighting with someone. We don't want to be caught in the crossfire.'

"But it could be Charles," Jane said. "Wait here. I'll go and check."

She ran around the corner, and the sight that met her there amazed her. She could see Charles sitting inside a cell, but his right foot had increased ten-fold in size! He had used the giant foot to kick open the door, effectively crushing the two guards between the outside of the cell door and the wall of the corridor.

Soon, Mr. Bennet came out from the cell. "Jane, where is your mother?"

His words awoke Jane from her stupor. "She is here!" she assured him, then ran back and called for her mother and sisters to join her.

When they came around the corner and saw Charles's big foot, their mouths gaped open, as if they were goldfish.

Charles raised his body and rested his weight on the big foot, leaning against the wall. "Let's get out of here." He limped, and every step was like an earthquake, shaking the floor. "I'll go first."

***

On the other side of the capital, General Fitzwilliam, the Darcy family and Sir Lewis were on board invisible cruisers which the General had procured through the black market. Their plan was to confront Prince Wickham by storming the floating palace from the north and the west.

Disgruntled staff members from the palace, who had joined the RA recently, promised to open the servant entrances for them. Richard had also obtained a detailed floor plan of the floating palace. They would need to force their way in through the laundry quarter and the chapel, where security was the lightest.

"Richard, our contact is not responding to signals," Darcy reported to his cousin via a secret communication channel on board his cruiser. "I'm going to head north by north-west 310 for the church."

"I'm in through the south," Richard replied. "Be careful. I'll meet you at the grand ballroom."

"Will do," Darcy replied as Georgiana amended the cruiser's course to the church.

"Shall we go in via the pulpit's clergy entrance?" Georgiana asked her brother.

"Go beneath the building," Sir Lewis said quietly. "There is a secret passage under the communion railing."

"That isn't shown on the floor plan," Elizabeth said. "How do you know about it, Uncle Lewis?"

"Catherine and I helped to build the church when I was the Genesis Director," Sir Lewis replied. "She added that entrance without my knowing about it, at first. When I confronted her about it, she said it would be useful for any clergy who felt sick during the service. I suspected she had other motives, but what was done was done, so I didn't make a big fuss about it. Nevertheless, it was never added to the floor plan."

"You know the co-ordinates?" Georgiana asked.

"No." Sir Lewis shook his head. "But it's marked by a C at the northern wall of the church, to stand for Catherine."

"We'll scan for it, once I go under the church," Darcy said.

They waited silently as the cruiser made its way toward its target.

"There it is!" Elizabeth pointed as a golden C appeared on the monitor.

"Lock onto the target," Darcy commanded, and Georgiana fired a stellar flair at the C. The door broke open upon impact, and she guided the cruiser in slowly.

Right and left, left and right, the cruiser navigated the winding passages without meeting any resistance, until they reached the end.

"The cruiser can't go through any farther," Sir Lewis said. The four of them gathered their ammunition, left the ship, and prepared to climb a flight of spiralling stairs by the landing area.

"Let me go up first," Darcy said, clearly wanting to protect his family.

"No, let me," Sir Lewis countered. "I still remember the direction. We need to turn a few times before we reach ground level."

Darcy nodded and followed him close by, with Georgiana and Elizabeth at the back.

After several minutes of twists and turns, they reached a door.

"This will open under the communion table." Sir Lewis murmured. He prepared to shoot it open, but Darcy stopped him.

"Let Georgiana work on the password," he suggested. "We don't want to alarm anyone."

Georgiana attached her watch to the door's keypad panel, typed in a few characters, and waited. After several seconds, the door slid open.

When they emerged, however, they were surprised by what they saw.

"Someone has changed the church!" Sir Lewis said.

The scene in front of their eyes was a church no more. Instead, they saw row after row of computers, and many doors and newly erected walls.

With the help of a navigator, they ran towards the southern side, where the main entrance of the church had originally been constructed, knowing that it should lead them into the heart of the palace. However, after two turns in the corridor, they were confronted by several armed guards, who opened fire at the sight of them.

"Stay close!" Darcy yelled as he fired back at the guards.

Boom!

Blast!

Bang!

As Darcy traded fire with the guards, he bit his lip, worrying about Elizabeth and Logan. Ducking and firing, he backed away into a green room...where he met face-to-face with Wickham!

"What are you doing here?" Wickham demanded, continuing to type rapidly on a computer keyboard.

When a shot from Darcy's laser revolver hit the final guard chasing him, and he pivoted to fire at the computer, not wanting Wickham to finish what he was doing.

Sparks flew.

"Bloody hell!" Wickham jumped away from the machine and ran to press a button on the wall. A panel slid open, revealing several laser longswords. He snatched one and whirled to strike the revolver from Darcy's hand.

Darcy yelled in pain and charged Wickham, shouldering him aside and grabbing another longsword from the wall cabinet.

Wickham parried, nearly hitting him on the head. As he ducked, he thrust the laser longsword at Wickham's waist.

The Prince jumped back, and their swords crossed several times. As they traded blow after blow around the room, Darcy managed to disarm Wickham with a heavy left-handed punch.

Wickham fell heavily backwards against the wall. Suddenly, a green glass partition emerged from the panelling and wrapped around him, effectively trapping him inside a glass chamber.

Darcy saw him yell as green smoke billowed up within the chamber.

Darcy tried to force open the partition, but it didn't move. He saw Wickham point at the computer, banging on the glass madly. Struck by the other man's panic, he turned to look at the slightly damaged computer as Georgiana, Elizabeth and Sir Lewis dashed in.

"What is happening?" Elizabeth asked. "Your hand is bleeding." She ran to his side to help him.

"Georgie, Wickham is trapped," Darcy said urgently. "Can you unlock the partition?"

Georgiana sat down at the computer and began typing frantically. But as they watched on, they saw Wickham go limp inside the chamber as the green smoke became heavier. Finally it covered the whole of his body, obscuring their view.

After several minutes, Georgiana succeeded in her efforts at the computer. With an eerie sound, the glass partition opened and Wickham tumbled out, face down, onto the floor.

Everyone in the room gaped as they saw that his red Princely uniform had dissolved, leaving him buck naked.

Darcy knelt to check on him. "He's alive."

As Darcy turned Wickham over, Sir Lewis said in confusion, "I thought it was Prince Wickham, inside there. How did he become a Princess?"

Darcy and Elizabeth looked at each other, unable to speak. Georgiana was flabbergasted; she typed another string of symbols into the computer, scrutinised the read-out, and exclaimed, "It's a genetic engineering machine! It must have been damaged by the gun fire. The gender-changing program was activated while he was trapped inside the chamber."

"So Wickham is a woman now!" Sir Lewis said.

Voting Options

1) Caroline causes problems

2) Anne demands her husband back

3) **Sir Lewis confronts the Queen Immortal** √

CHAPTER ELEVEN

Soon thereafter, General Fitzwilliam and his troop arrived. Darcy advised him immediately about the latest development, and Richard instructed his men to take Wickham to a medical room for treatment and observation.

"Did you find Aunt Catherine and Anne?" Georgiana asked.

"They are in the medical room, too," Richard replied.

When they arrived there, they saw that the Queen Immortal, was lying there, motionless, with several beams of red rays pointing at various parts of her body.

Anne stood up when she saw the group entering. "Father, how are you?" She walked slowly to Sir Lewis and took his hand.

Sir Lewis looked back at her and whispered, "I'm well. And you?"

Anne nodded.

He smoothed his hands over her hair and face. "You have grown up."

"Yes. I was only ten when you disappeared."

"Disappeared?"

"Do you not remember?"

"Remember?"

"It was the twenty-eighth of May. We had a dinner and, later, you tucked me in. The next day, when I asked Mama, she said you had gone out to attend to some urgent business...but you were not seen, ever again – until now!"

"The twenty-eighth of May? I tucked you in?" Sir Lewis frowned, struggling to remember.

"The twenty-eighth of May was my mother's birthday," Georgiana said softly.

Sir Lewis turned to look at her. "Yes, it was Sweetie's birthday." He looked back at his daughter and his sick wife. Then, suddenly, his frown lifted and he said, "After I put Anne to bed, I went back to my room to have a drink, to drown my sorrow. I was remembering my Anne. And, when I woke up the next day, I found myself in the 'Heart.'"

"Oh, Papa!" Anne wrapped her arms around him and sobbed.

"Could it be Aunt Catherine who sent you there?" Richard said.

"We won't know that unless she wakes up," Darcy added.

As he spoke, Bingley, whose foot had returned to normal, entered the room, accompanied by the Bennets. Elizabeth hurried over to hug her family.

"Mom, Dad, are you well?"

"Yes, considering the situation," Mr. Bennet replied.

"Lizzy, you will be the death of me! Why did you have to rebel against the Queen Immortal? Why?" Mrs. Benet looked down and gasped. "Your belly is glowing!"

Everyone turned to look at Elizabeth, who blush bright red. "Mama, I'm pregnant."

"Oh my lord, don't tell me that the andudas conducted experiments on you as they did on our cousin Collins? Whatever will we do?" Mrs. Bennet burst into tears.

Darcy stepped forward. "Mrs. Bennet, Elizabeth and I were married on Hartfield. And you do not have to be worried. Logan is my baby. He glows because of some radioactive dates we ate on Hartfield."

Elizabeth's sisters were concerned. They buzzed about, congratulating her and asking her a hundred questions. Standing apart, her mother fanned herself and said, "Oh, Lizzy, you're such a smart girl! And so wealthy now! So many estates in the Planet! Was that why you invited him to the mating capsule? To seduce him?"

Mom and Dad, can you ask Grandma to shut up? Her shrill voice is hurting my ears.

Elizabeth and Darcy listened to Logan's mind-voice and shook their heads, not sure whether to laugh or simply roll their eyes.

Sir Lewis appeared to have heard Logan's mind talk, as well. He glared at Mrs. Bennet and said to her husband, "Can you all leave the room?"

Elizabeth urged her family to rest in a more comfortable chamber, and General Fitzwilliam assigned men to escort them out.

After the Bennets and Bingley left, Darcy turned to his cousin. "Richard, did you manage to locate your parents?"

The General shook his head. "My men are still scouting the palace. We haven't found the seal yet, either. Without the seal, we cannot legally take over the administration. Anne, do you have any ideas?"

But Anne's reply was not helpful, either. "I don't know. Before the wedding, Wickham was very charming and kind. He told me that he would find a way to cure Mother's illness. Since the wedding, though, I haven't seen much of him. I've been here with Mother, most of the time. I only heard about the persecution and the arrests very recently. When I tried to talk to him, his men always came up with excuses. I managed to track him down at Matlock, when he was hurting Georgiana. I confronted him when we returned to the Palace. But he was furious. He slapped me, and I've been locked up in this room, ever since."

"But you were with him on the televised broadcast," Darcy said with a frown.

"What broadcast?" Anne asked.

"Wickham gave us an ultimatum, via the galaxy television – surrender or he would kill my family," Elizabeth told her.

"But that's impossible. I haven't seen him since we returned from Matlock House."

"Bloody Wickham! He must have doctored the broadcast, to make it appear that he had Anne and Catherine by his side. If he hadn't already been turned into a woman, I would strangle him for hitting you," Sir Lewis said.

Anne stared at him. "What do you mean, 'turned into a woman'?"

"I'm sorry," Georgiana said gently. "He got into a fight with Fitzwilliam and ended up in a gender transformation chamber."

"Oh my goodness!" Anne sat down heavily, with her hand over her mouth.

"We will demand an annulment," her father said. "You're better off without him."

"So what do we do now?" Elizabeth asked.

"I will check on Wickham again," Georgiana said, "I think there are some medical procedures that can hasten his recovery."

Sir Lewis decided to stay with his daughter, at his wife's bedside. He wanted answers, when the Queen Immortal finally woke up. In turn, Georgiana and Elizabeth went to check on Wickham, while Darcy followed Richard to the administration wing of the palace.

Mrs. Bennet and her three daughters decided to rest in the royal chambers of the Queen and King. They tried out the luxurious furniture and all of the gadgets that had not been damaged in the fighting. Mr. Bennet had wandered off to the library.

Bingley pulled Jane into another room, where they sank down on a sofa.

"So...you have an implanted big foot." Jane eyed his legs, which had turned back to their normal size.

Bingley blushed and nodded. "I don't like people knowing that."

"Why?"

"Kids laughed at me at school when they learned about the secret. They said I should be bigger somewhere else."

"Oh!" she said, then smiled. "But you're not bad in that 'somewhere else' either, you know."

"Now that I'm grown up."

She smiled and kissed his cheek. "And I am glad of that. But this big foot 'feature'... can that pass on to your children, if we are allowed to have children in future?"

"I'd love to have a bunch of kids with you," he said, and kissed her back. "But it's only an implant, not something I can pass on to my children."

"But why did your parents do that – implant you with an expandable big foot."

He looked away. "...It's kind of stupid."

"We shouldn't have any secret," Jane urged gently.

Bingley sighed. "Just so. Well, my family is from new money. My parents built their fortune from scratch, so they were anxious for their children to be 'superior'. When they had Louisa, they couldn't afford medical enhancement for the baby. But by the time they had Caroline, they had more money than they knew how to spend, and so they decided to 'enhance' her. After that, of course, I was born, and they decided that I should be enhanced, as well. I never understand why they chose such a stupid enhancement as a big foot. Dad said he ticked the wrong implant for me when he was filling out the form, and mom said he was a miser and got a shonky lab to do it."

"Well, it certainly did us some good, today! You were magnificent, saving all of my family." She wrapped her arms around him.

Bingley was about to return her embrace when he thought of something. "Speaking of my sister," he said darkly, "I need to find her."

"Why?"

"She surrendered us to that bloody Wickham. I'm her only brother."

"That was Mr. Darcy and General Fitzwilliam's plan anyway."

"Still! How could she choose the reward over family? I have had enough of her attitude and interference. This time, she crossed the line. I know some distant relatives on Hartfield who work with Andudas. I will find Caroline and send her there, for the rest of her life."

"Charles, you shouldn't be too harsh with her."

"But she betrayed me, simply because she doesn't like your family. How could she do that to her only brother? What if I had been tortured or killed?"

"You weren't. It has been a strange and difficult time, with this evil Prince Wickham threatening the peace. Please try to be forgiving."

"You are truly too good." Bingley gave her another kiss. "All right, I will settle on sending her to spend a year at the Andudas outpost."

Jane nodded her agreement, and Bingley grinned, deciding not to tell her that the outpost didn't have any 'human' facilities – no beds, no bathroom, no shower, not even toilet paper. Caroline would live in the wild, with all the mud and dirt that wilderness living entailed, once he got his hands on her. If she didn't go willingly, he would retaliate and gave *her* some sleeping pills!

***

In a different chamber in the medical room, Georgiana checked on Wickham's vital. He wasn't restrained.

"I think I will pump more female hormone into his breathing apparatus. Since he accidentally triggered the procedure, his hormone levels are not normal."

"Are you sure you know what you're doing?" Elizabeth asked, frowning. "Shouldn't we wait for the army doctors to administer that?"

"I've been helping Uncle Lewis with his brain wave stabilization, and studying the human body for these past weeks. You know I'm a geek when it comes to learning," Georgiana said. She touched a few keys on the console and Darcy and the General appeared before them. "Richard, where are the army doctors? I think Wickham's hormone level is unbalanced. That may be why he's still in a coma. Can someone take a look at him?"

"They are busy attending to the casualties in and around the palace. Do whatever you deem right. You've already been acting as a doctor for the Alliance for several days." The General had no time for the likes of Wickham. He was sure he could find his parents and the seal without Wickham's help.

Georgiana allowed herself a satisfied smile and switched off the screen, happy to know that they trusted her ability.

While she was busy calculating the hormone to be used on Wickham, the door to the chamber burst open. "Where is my brother?" A high-pitched voice demanded, shattering her concentration.

Georgiana and Elizabeth turned to see an elegantly dressed Caroline Bingley striding into the room.

"Oooh, Georgie, I'm so happy to see you! Where have you been? Are you well? Where is Mr. Darcy?" Caroline exclaimed, and hugged Georgiana enthusiastically, nearly knocking her off her chair.

Georgiana put one hand to the console to steady herself. Before she could say a word, Caroline continued her babbling. "That horrible Prince Wickham claimed that all of you were rebels. I'm sure he was just making up excuses. He must be working with that Eliza. She's a whore, tricking Darcy into a mating capsule and keeping him there on Hartfield. I pretended to help the Prince so that I could stay in the Palace and investigate."

"Caroline!" Georgiana said in a loud voice to quiet her down. "Fitzwilliam and Elizabeth are married. She's no whore."

"Hello, Caroline. Long time no see," Elizabeth greeted in her usual sarcastic manner. "I see that you're still just as polite as you were in Hertfordshire."

"Darcy is married?" Caroline's eyes widened and her voice became shrill. "To *her*?" She slapped her hand down onto the console. "Georgie, you must be joking! Why would he want her when he could have *me*? I am Caroline Bingley of Netherfield! I'm more elegant. I dress and walk with much better taste than this whor..."

Slap!

"Ouch!" Rubbing her cheek, Caroline turned to Elizabeth angrily. "You're a witch! How did you manage to hit me without touching me?" She jumped towards her rival and raised her hand, intending to slap Elizabeth's face in retaliation. But before she could do so, she felt a sharp kick on her shin.

"Ouch!" She doubled over, steadying herself against the console with one hand while she held onto her leg with the other. But, not a second later, she jerked away from the console, as a spark of electricity sizzled and shocked her body. "My head! My leg! They hurt!"

"Logan!" Elizabeth gasped.

I didn't do anything to her head. I only kicked her leg. She said you were a whore, Logan explained in mind talk.

Elizabeth folded her hands across her abdomen, not wanting her child to hurt Caroline any more. "Logan, it's not right to hit a woman."

But she wanted to hurt you! he argued. *I'm sure Father would want me to protect you. If she comes near you again, I'll still kick her.*

"We will talk about this with your father." She shook her head, not sure how to calm her stubborn boy.

"Oh, Georgie, you're my witness that this woman is crazy. She talks to herself. Who is this Logan?" Caroline leaned on the console and breathed heavily with pain.

"Logan is my nephew." Georgiana couldn't suppress her smile. She had wanted to slap this annoying woman many times, in the past, when Caroline was fawning all over her brother. Now Georgie wished she could give Logan a pat on the head. Instead, after seeing Elizabeth's exasperated expression, she turned away. When her gaze focused on the monitor, she exclaimed, "Get away from the console, Caroline!"

"What?" Caroline jumped away as she was told.

"Oh no!" Georgiana cradled her head in her hands. "You've messed up my formula, and now we've pumped too much female hormone into Wickham."

Everyone turned their gaze to the woman lying on the bed, who was literally growing in certain areas, bursting the medical gown he was wearing. Wickham now had larger breasts, a more voluptuous figure, and longer hair. Her body moved. She blinked her long lashes, opened her eyes and peered up at the three women standing near her bedside.

"Oh! Where have all the men gone?" She spoke in a soft voice, and smoothed her hands over her body. "I want a man."

The three women standing there stared, open-mouthed. Elizabeth was the first to react, since she certainly didn't want Logan to hear or see any more. Could Logan see things yet? She shook her head, pulled a body suit from the cabinet, and threw it over Wickham's body.

"Cover yourself," she ordered sharply, and headed for the door. "Georgie, I will go and wait outside now. Call Fitzwilliam and Richard, and ask them what to do."

Georgiana tried to help Wickham into the body suit, but the newly transformed female was too womanly for the suit Elizabeth had grabbed. Georgiana found a blanket and covered Wickham up, then called her brother and cousin again.

"Who is she?" Caroline asked, her eyes still wide as she took in the sight of Wickham's amazing figure under the blanket.

"I have a problem here," Georgiana said briskly to the image on her computer monitor.

"Your brother isn't here. What's it?" Richard asked, raising his head from his work.

"Oh, what a handsome man!" Wickham exclaimed. Throwing off the blanket, she stood up and swayed in front of the console. "My dear, you look very strong. Come to me now. I want you desperately."

Richard looked at her naked form with wide eyes and then asked Georgiana, "Is that Wickham?"

Georgiana nodded while Caroline stuttered, "Prince Wickham?"

"What did you do to him?" Richard asked, his eyes trying to look somewhere other than at Wickham.

"It's her," Georgiana said with a sigh. "Caroline touched the wrong buttons and altered up the hormone calculation. Now he has too much female hormone."

"Can you...reverse it?" Richard asked, his voice becoming hoarse. He was still a man, after all. No matter how disgusting Wickham's actions had been, his new-formed body could still turn any man on.

"I don't think it's wise to try. His body may not be able to withstand any more genetic transformation." Georgiana managed to find a wraparound medical gown, and hastened to cover Wickham up. "What should I do with her?"

"Just give me a few men." Wickham tried to push her away and untie the gown again.

Richard nodded towards the chair on the side to Georgiana.

Understanding his meaning, she led the protesting Wickham to the chair, pressed the button immediately, and strapped him there.

"What are you doing?" Wickham screamed. "Let me go! I want a man!"

Moving deftly, Georgiana injected him with a sedative. He stopped the struggling and looked at her groggily.

"Let me interrogate him," Richard said. "Wickham, where are Lord and Lady Matlock?"

"Wickham?" the captive replied. "Who's Wickham?"

"You don't remember?" Richard continued.

"Remember what?"

"What is your name?"

Wickham tilted his head and thought hard. "I'm Caroline Bingley of Netherfield. I'm more elegant. I dress and walk with much better taste than this whor..."

Georgiana looked at the console and cradled her head in her hands again, while the real Caroline recoiled in outrage.

"Shit! The electricity spark! Caroline, this is your own fault. You started the brain connection program, too. Now Wickham shares some your brain history. He's —"

"I remember now! I want to become the Mistress of Pemberley!" announced 'Princess' Wickham, in a sophisticated tone that rivalled that of Miss Bingley.

"No, *I* want to be Mistress of Pemberley!" Caroline retorted. "You're sick."

"I'm elegant, well-educated and well-endowed. Darcy will want me more than you, you flat-chested country chit!" Princess Wickham replied.

"Georgiana, can you put both of them to sleep?" General Fitzwilliam said.

"Georgiana Darcy?" Princess Wickham's eyes suddenly became dark with hatred, and she spoke in a low, deep voice that reminded everyone of her former self. "I'll kill you!"

Caroline shrank from this mad woman, and quietly slipped out of the room.

Seeing Wickham's sudden recollection of his previous life, Richard seized the chance and asked, "Where are Lord and Lady Matlock?"

Wickham laughed and replied, "They were on their way to a camp on Hartfield, to be turned into animals. The high and mighty Lord Matlock will soon be a crocodile! Or perhaps a bear! That would punish him for treating me like nobody throughout my youth."

Richard looked at the twisted woman-man with wonder. How could so much hatred be bottled up inside one person? What had the Darcy and Fitzwilliam families done to him, to make him so sick in the mind? But he had no time for compassion. He had to get the most out of the creature while it still remembered being Wickham.

"And where is the planetary seal?"

"You will never find it. Earth will fall into anarchy without its ruling royalty. The stupid old mare has paved the way for this world's chaos. The so-called Queen Immortal has suppressed us for too long. You'll never find the seal!" Wickham insisted, shouting until her voice was hoarse. Then she dropped her head, seemingly exhausted until she raised it again and said, in a voice similar to Caroline Bingley's, "Perhaps I'll agree to tell you where the seal is if you convince Darcy to divorce that whore and marry me!"

The General gave his cousin a nod, and Georgiana quickly jabbed a needle into the patient's arm again.

Wickham screamed aloud, "Don't hurt me. I'd tell you where the seal is. I just want to marry Darcy. I want Darcy. I want Darcy. I want Darcy…" When her voice faltered to a stop, Georgiana was relieved. She was not sure whether her patient's brain could handle these two tortured mental memories.

"Georgie, I need to organise a rescue mission to Hartfield now," Richard said. "I'll talk to you later about how to extract the seal's location from Wickham."

She nodded. "Perhaps we can organise a fake wedding between Fitzwilliam and Wickham." She felt the need to lighten the atmosphere. The past few weeks had been horrible, and if they failed to find the seal or rescue her uncle and aunt in time, the future would be even worse. But her dark attempt at humour sounded crazy even to her own ears.

General Fitzwilliam shook his head and shut down the communication.

Voting Options

1) Some one travels to Hartfield √

2) Wickham's new mission

3) Where is the seal?

CHAPTER TWELVE

Elizabeth wandered through the floating palace, searching for her husband while mind-talking with little Logan Darcy.

"You shouldn't hit a woman," Elizabeth said.

"Even if the woman is evil?" Her abdomen gleamed as Logan made his presence known. "Isn't that a form of discrimination? I think we should treat men and women the same."

She sighed heavily, pondering how to explain chivalry to her unborn son until, at last, she reached the grand ballroom. At least, that is what she thought the room had originally been, judging by its size. Now, however, it had been transformed into a giant surveillance centre. Every inch of the wall was covered with monitors, showing major strategic locations throughout the Planet.

"Wow!"

What's up, Mom?

"It looks as though Prince Wickham has been trying to become Big Brother."

What's Big Brother? Logan asked, then continued, *Oh, yes. I remember hearing on the galaxynet about that. Has this wicked prince been monitoring his empire, trying to suppress people's free thinking?*

"More or less. This giant room has so many computers in it that I've lost count. Now, back to what you've just done. You shouldn't hit Miss Bingley, nor any person, nor any animals. But especially you shouldn't hit women, because they tend to have a weaker physique. That's why, in Earth history, men give special treatment to women."

That's bullshit.

"Logan Darcy!"

I'm sorry, Mom. Logan dimmed his shine. *But I hear that Uncle Richard swore like this all the time.*

"You shouldn't imitate people's bad habits. I don't want a disrespectful, vulgar child. If you do such a thing again..." Elizabeth hesitated, biting her lip as she tried to think of a way to punish Logan while he was still within her. "I'll...stay away from any foods that you like!"

No, Mom! Logan wailed. *I love blueberry ice cream. Please Mom, please don't stop eating it.*

Elizabeth rolled her eyes. She had wondered why she'd developed such a sudden fancy for the frozen treat. At this rate, her belly would have a bluesy radiance soon. "Well, at least you apologised. This time, I will let it go."

Thanks, Mom, Logan said, then asked in a serious tone, *If wickedness is all the same, if it's done by a man and a woman, what can we do?*

"Violence is a kind of wickedness, too. We shouldn't use it on anyone. We should try to find a peaceful, non-violent way to resolve problems."

I don't think it'll work. We're at war here.

"We're not at war." Elizabeth shook her head. Logan only had the mind of a three-year-old. He was too young to contemplate these sorts of questions about life. She wished he could be born a 'normal' child, with a love of fun and a cheerful disposition. "We're just organizing a rescue."

A rescue that used weapons and caused bloodshed. Her body glittered again. Logan's mind was full of argument.

Suddenly, Elizabeth heard other voices in the room: "Is that Elizabeth Bennet?" "Why is she talking to herself?"

She looked around. The voices were definitely not from someone in the room. Rather, they sounded as if they were coming over a microphone. Could the people on the streets see her?

She decided to reply. "Yes, I'm Elizabeth Bennet. I'm in the grand ballroom of the floating palace."

A round of loud cheers sounded, as if an immense crowd of people were cheering and celebrating.

"Miss Bennett, Commander Frederick Wentworth from Monkford here."

She straightened in surprise. "Are you on Planet Monkford now?"

"Actually, no. I'm in Times Square, New York. Dignitaries from all over the galaxy were invited by Prince Wickham to come and witness the execution of the – the rebels. You're being beamed to the widescreen TV here."

Elizabeth's gaze scrolled along the rows of monitors. The grand ballroom must also serve as Prince Wickham's television studio. Elizabeth could see herself on nearly all of the monitors. The monitors seemed to be arranged in alphabetical orders, by country and then city. She finally found the screen for New York: Times Square.

"Wow!" She was at a loss for words. It looked as though literally millions of people had gathered there, and a giant screen on top of a building was showing an image of her, as she now stood in this room in the palace.

"Of course, many of us don't agree with this Prince, who came from nowhere and started persecuting noblemen and later gentry too. So we gather here mostly to see if the Resistance Alliance can take the palace."

"Why did I suddenly hear your voices?"

"A few of the guests decided to...explore. We found a computer that seemed to link to the widescreen, and now we seem to have found a way to connect the audio, as well. Were you talking to your unborn baby?"

The loud cheers suddenly turned silence, as if all of the people in Times Square were holding their breath, waiting to hear her answer.

Yes, I'm Logan Darcy. Delighted to make your acquaintance, Commander Wentworth, Logan said in an excited voice, sounding as adult as a three-year-old could. And his excitement seemed to be transformed into glimmer as Elizabeth's shinning abdomen turned multi-coloured. She was stunned to see the image of herself with a shining belly on the Times Square jumbotron.

"So the rumour is true! You're now married to the Queen Immortal's nephew, Fitzwilliam Darcy. But this Logan Darcy is your unborn baby. You can talk to him while he's still inside your body, and he glows?"

Yes! Smart one, Commander! Logan replied gleefully. Of course, no one could hear him. Elizabeth felt him move, too, as if he were doing a somersault inside of her. Could a baby that small make such a move? She was totally confused about what Logan could or could not do. She thought it was best to be honest.

"Yes, I married Fitzwilliam Darcy on Planet Hartfield. We were trapped inside the core of the planet for some weeks and ate some radioactive dates. They seems to have sped up the brain development of my unborn baby. Logan can talk to me via mind talk, and he glitters when he's excited."

"What a phenomenon!" "Awesome!" "I'd be worried." Murmurs of all kinds were heard from the many people surrounding Command Wentworth.

"Watch out!"

Wentworth's sudden loud warning made Elizabeth's hair stand up. On the jumbotron view, she saw, as if in slow motion, that someone was attacking her from behind with a schiavona, an ancient sword made of some shimmering substance. She jumped away just in time to prevent a slash to her skull, but her right shoulder was hit.

"Ah!" She cried out in pain, and looked down at the burning flesh. Taking out her revolver, she prepared to fire at the assailant – then froze when she discovered who it was.

"Lydia! What are you doing?"

"Agent Lydia," she replied in a calm, level voice that was totally unlike her usual exuberant 15 year old self. "I kill all Bennets, Darcys, Fitzwilliams and anyone else who is an enemy, as instructed by Prince Wickham." She raised the sword and swung it again at Elizabeth.

Not wanting to shoot her own sister, Elizabeth moved nimbly to avoid Lydia's potentially lethal blows. "What are you thinking?" Elizabeth cried out. "Has Wickham brainwashed you?"

"Agent Lydia was programmed by Prince Wickham," came the wooden reply, "to serve him in whatever way he deemed useful."

Lydia was dressed in a shoulder-to-floor robe that was similar to Wickham's, but in black. Her deadly, robotic expression, combined with her methodical slashing of blow after blow at her elder sister, made Lydia seem like an inhuman demon.

Bit by bit, Elizabeth was backed into a corner. She found that she had nowhere else to run, and was pondering how to avoid the next blow, but her assailant suddenly staggered backwards.

Yes! Logan cheered.

"Logan!" Elizabeth cried out. She wasn't sure whether to reprimand her son for fighting Lydia or thank him for saving her life.

But Lydia was already back with a vengeance. She raised her sword and groaned out loud, preparing to hit Elizabeth again.

While Elizabeth tried to avoid the blows and looked for weapon, Logan kicked Lydia again. It quickly became clear to Elizabeth that she was now in a sort of protective shield. Every time Lydia came near, she was driven away by Logan's kicks. Each time this happened, the brightness of Elizabeth's body changed colour, as Logan celebrated his success at protecting his mother. And the entire fight was captured on camera, broadcast live all over the galaxy.

Finally, with Logan's help, Elizabeth backed Lydia into opposite corner of the room and disarmed her younger sister. But when she tried to twist Lydia's arm and tie her up, Lydia lashed out and scratched her face, loosening Elizabeth's hold. The assailant took advantage and pressed her hand to the wall. A panel slid open, and Lydia slipped through the gap in the wall, disappearing as it closed behind her.

Elizabeth moved her hand along the wall, pressing, trying to find the button or device that could open the panel so that she could chase after Lydia. But it was no use.

"Mrs. Darcy, are you hurt?" a woman's voice called with concern.

Elizabeth abandoned the search and turned back to look at the monitor of Times Square again. The image of herself still dominated the giant screen there.

"I am Catherine Moreland, Ambassador from United Galaxy Commission. Are you all right?"

"I'm fine," Elizabeth said breathlessly. "Thank you, Miss Moreland."

"But your shoulder is bleeding."

Elizabeth took out the miniature first aid kit that she wore at her waist and pressed the palm-size device on her shoulder. It sealed the wound and stopped the bleeding immediately.

"People in the Square have been discussing the future on Earth." Moreland said.

"Oh!"

"Some people here are in favour of getting rid of the monarchy altogether and setting up a republic."

Elizabeth nodded, but she was unsure whether this was a good time to make drastic changes, after a time of such turmoil.

"We don't want the Queen!" a crowd of people began to chant. "We don't want the noblemen and women!"

"The psyches are bad, too!" someone else added. "Wickham was a Tea-Leaf Reader."

"I think Logan Darcy is cool!" a female voice interjected.

"But he's Fitzwilliam Darcy's son!" another countered.

"What's wrong with that? Mr. Darcy rebelled against his aunt."

"And Darcy and Elizabeth fought against the ridiculous laws on Earth so that they could love each. They are courageous!"

"Yes, and Logan is special. He glows, and he protected his mother from that robotic killer."

"We should make him our president!"

"Logan Darcy, Planet Earth's president!"

"President Logan Darcy!"

The discussion, argument and cheers grew louder in Times Square. As Elizabeth scanned other monitors, she could see people scribbling hastily and holding up signs. Wave after wave of signs with "President Logan Darcy" were appearing on the screens.

I would be honoured, Logan told his mother.

But Elizabeth shook her head and addressed the bank of screens. "Dear fellow citizens, thank you for the honour of your high opinion. But Logan has yet to be born. I am confident that the Resistance Alliance will consult the citizens concerning how Earth should be governed, once matters in the palace have been sorted out."

"You could be President Pro Tempore for now, until Mr. Logan comes of age."

"Yes, President Elizabeth Darcy!"

"We'd like that. A female president."

"But will she become like the old queen?"

Elizabeth cleared her throat, and the throng stilled. "Dear citizens, please do not give me any title or official duty. I just want to be a good wife and a good mother. Maybe, after Logan is grown up, I will return to work. I enjoy working with computers. But politics is beyond me," Elizabeth told them firmly.

Mom, you should take it, Logan argued. *You could help a lot of people, being the president.*

"Elizabeth!" Darcy hurried into the room at that moment. "What happened?" Spotting her wound and torn space suit with concern, he came to wrap his arms around her protectively.

"It's Lydia. Wickham seems to have brainwashed her," Elizabeth explained, returning his embrace.

Yes! I have a robotic killer aunt, Logan commented. *And a President mother!*

"A president? What's Logan talking about?"

"Mr. Darcy, I am Catherine Moreland, Ambassador from United Galaxy Commission. It seems that citizens from around the globe want to elect your special son as the President of Earth. But for the meantime, as he has yet to be born and grow up, they have settled upon your wife, Elizabeth Darcy."

Darcy looked at Elizabeth with wide eyes.

She pointed to the monitors on the wall. It seemed now that all showed signs that read, "President Elizabeth," "President Mrs. Darcy," "President Elizabeth Darcy," or "Logan Darcy's President Mother," in one form or another.

Darcy was lost for words for a second. Then he released her and clasped Elizabeth's hand instead.

"Thank you, Miss Moreland. And thank you all, dear citizens. My family is thankful for all your support. We are happy to have stopped the execution of innocent people by taking control of the palace. To protect the future of Earth, General Fitzwilliam of the Resistant Alliance is on a mission to Planet Hartfield. According to Wickham, the official seal was sent there."

"We can't carry on without a government for long," one voice said.

"Mr. Darcy, I think that citizen is correct," Ambassador Moreland said. "We have dignitaries from over 130 planets here. Perhaps we can help you organise a quick referendum for the interim government."

"Commander Wentworth of Planet Monkford here. Judging by the wishes of the people," Commander Wentworth said, "one proposal we have to put forward is for your wife, Mrs. Darcy, to become President Pro Tempore of Planet Earth. She and your son just fought off a killer, in front of billions of people. And she also modestly refused the job. People won't see her as another potential Queen Immortal."

Darcy looked at Elizabeth, who was shaking her head in negation. But her body was in techno-colour, and Logan was chanting, *Mother President!*

"Thank you Commander and Ambassador. Might we ask the dignitaries to come to the palace? Citizen, we promise to be open in our discussions. I will invite some of the RA personnel to come and help, on site, so that representatives from each city can speak out during the discussion. Shall we reconvene here in five hours time? Good. Thank you," Darcy said, bowed, and escorted his wife out of the grand ballroom.

That was exciting! Logan said.

"Logan, I mean it," Elizabeth said. "I don't want to be a president, and have to be involved in politics every day."

Maybe they find you a good prime minister. Then you would only need to visit children's hospitals and ice-cream shops, Logan reasoned.

Darcy interceded. "Son, be a good boy. Your mother is injured. We don't want her to stress out. I'm taking her to the doctor, and she needs her rest. So do you."

Umh, Logan yawned. *Yes, Father. Will you rock Mother and me to sleep? Your love-making rhythm is good for me.*

"Logan!" Elizabeth cried out in frustration.

"Fine, Mother! I'll shut up."

"He has the brain of more than a three-year-old!" she complained.

"Perhaps he's grown more, in the past few days. We will ask the doctor to check on him."

NO! Logan protested. *I hate needles.*

"The doctor isn't using needles on your skin yet," Elizabeth said. "It's my skin that takes the pinch." She turned to her husband and said soberly, "We need to send out alerts about Lydia."

Darcy nodded and gave instruction to the RA members via his ring.

Voting Options
1) The killer strikes again
2) The past is dug up √
3) The chase is on

CHAPTER THIRTEEN

When Darcy and Elizabeth arrived at the medical room, they were met with loud screams.

"Untie me immediately!" a woman's voice shrilled.

"It's my aunt," Darcy said, frowning. "She's woken up."

"Shut up, woman!" Sir Lewis' agitated voice could be heard, too.

They walked into the inner chamber and saw that Queen Catherine de Bourgh was pulling at the restraints on her wrists and ankles. Sir Lewis had his hands on the helmet he was wearing, a deep frown on his face, pacing around the room.

When the couple saw the Darcys, they both called out:

"Nephew, you're back and safe. Thank God! Untie me now." The Queen instructed.

"Elizabeth, help me quiet this mad woman down. She's giving me a headache." Sir Lewis complained, striding to Elizabeth's side.

Elizabeth led Sir Lewis to sit down, checked the read-out on his helmet, and pressed a few buttons to release a more intense electromagnetic wave to help calm him down. "Where are Anne and Georgiana, or the doctor?" she said in a soft voice.

At the same time, Darcy used the first aid kit that his wife had quietly passed to him and jabbed his aunt with a sedative shot. The Queen's loud bellow rose to a final height. "What did you do?!" Then her words trailed off to a slow, hoarse groan.

"The young girls left with the doctor," Sir Lewis said. "They are taking Princess Wickham to scout the palace for the seal."

"'Princess' Wickham? Scouting for the seal? What nonsense are you talking about?" Queen Immortal demanded.

"I thought General Fitzwilliam was going to Hartfield to locate it," Elizabeth said uncertainly, looking to her husband.

"That was what Richard told me, before I found you in that ballroom-turned-television-studio."

"Who is this woman?" The Queen Immortal's voice, lowered but still displeased, interrupted the discussion between the Darcys.

"This is my wife, the former Elizabeth Bennet of Hertfordshire."

"That woman! The one who lured you to the mating capsule Commander Collins told me about? Have you taken leave of your senses, Darcy? How could you marry such a low woman, of such inferior birth, with no connections or wealth? Are you lost to every feeling of propriety and delicacy? I am utterly ashamed of you!"

Elizabeth bit her lip and took a few deep breaths, reminding herself firmly that there was no need to argue with an opinionated old woman, especially one who was related to one's husband.

"Stop, Aunt!" Darcy snapped. "I will not permit you to abuse my wife." Darcy wrapped his hand around Elizabeth's waist. "My wife is a smart, compassionate, loving woman.

She's also the most beautiful female I've ever known. Her father comes from the Gentry Class, and so did mine. We are equal. I don't care about your horrid class distinctions anyway. I'm honoured that she has become my wife. She was a tower of strength during our ordeal in the centre of Hartfield. Since our wedding, we've been extremely happy."

"Her belly glows! She must be an alien in disguise, an evil creature. You know, every savage can reproduce! Darcy, you should never lower your standards. And what about my dear Anne? You're engaged to her. My sister and I planned this union while the two of you were still in your cradles. From your earliest hours, you were destined for your cousin. She has been waiting for you for so many years, trusting in your honour!"

"No, Aunt. Elizabeth is carrying my baby. She ate some radioactive dates, on Hartfield, and that's why the baby glitters. Anyway, Anne married Wickham." Elizabeth could feel the anger radiating from her husband's body. "While you were unconscious."

"And you're bull-shitting," Sir Lewis added flatly to Queen Catherine, "when you claim that my sweetie planned for Darcy and Anne's engagement. It's all in your crazy mind."

"Shut up, Lewis! I'm fed up with the way you pine for my sister. And besides, Anne could not possibly have married Wickham! He's not a whole man."

"You knew?" Darcy asked in surprised.

"I found Wickham drifting in the sea, nearly two years ago, when I was cruising along the coast in Brighton. He confided in me about his accident at the hands of a vicious madwoman who cut off his manly organ."

Elizabeth looked at her husband. Apparently Wickham had spun a story to win the Queen's sympathy, describing Georgiana as a vicious madwoman.

"And so you kept him close," Sir Lewis sneered. "In your bed, I'm sure."

"Nonsense! After he regained consciousness, I interviewed him. He's very smart and has the most brilliant ideas. I gave him a small position in the Genesis Department. But then he started using his tea-leaves to give me readings. And he was very accurate. He predicted that I would succeed to the throne after Queen Thorpe."

"Where *is* Queen Thorpe?" Sir Lewis asked. "Did you make her disappear, too?"

"She succumbed to a mysterious disease. I had nothing to do with it. It's absurd to accuse me of such a crime."

"So you had nothing to do with my disappearance to Hartfield?"

Hatred radiated from the Queen's eyes. "I would have done it myself, if I wasn't such a stickler to a sense of proprietary. I had nothing to do with your disappearance."

"I don't believe you," Sir Lewis stated.

"I don't care whether you believe me or not. You're just a pathetic man, living in the past with the image of my oh so lovely sister Anne."

"Stop bad-mouthing my sweetie!" Sir Lewis insisted, raising his voice.

"Why should I? Your sweetie was the poison in our relationship. We had three in that marriage."

"You are the man-eater. You destroyed our marriage with your countless affairs, very early on. I tried to love, honour and respect you, at the very beginning. But how can I give my heart to someone who sleeps with any willing man who crosses her path? When I saw how happy Anne and George Darcy were, how could I not feel miserable over my own stupidity?"

"You only married me because you couldn't have my sister. Despite all of your power in the Planet as the Director of the Genesis Department, Special Envoy to the Galaxy United Commission, the noblest heritage on Earth, with thousands years of history behind you, you couldn't compete with George Darcy, a mere farmer!"

Sir Lewis gripped the arms of the chair, almost cracking them. But he breathed deeply, in and out, before he spoke again. "And why did you marry me, if you thought I was such a feeble person?"

"You truly want to know? Well, why not. I didn't want my sister to have all the money and power in the world. She always got more attention from my parents, as a child, because she had this tiny bit of asthma. I'm convinced that it wasn't serious at all. It was just her tactic for keeping me away from my parents. And when she grew older and healthier, she attracted all the boys because she looked so vulnerable. Men are all stupid. They were duped by her, and they fell at her feet. Why couldn't they appreciate a strong woman like me? One with goals and drive? I couldn't allow her to marry, prosper and gloat for long. And I rejoiced in her early death."

"She harbours a great deal of hatred toward your mother," Elizabeth whispered sadly to Darcy, who was tightening his fists.

"You're insane!" Sir Lewis said to his wife. "Your jealousy knows no bounds. For no better reason than that, you turned me into a pawn in your life. You got me drunk and deliberately got pregnant."

"And you were calling out for Anne Darcy all the time. You're the one who's wretched."

"It wasn't enough that you shackled me with your vicious self? You had to get rid of me, too?"

"I had nothing to do with that. But I'm surely glad of it. You're useless. There were so many opportunities in the administration. If you'd spent your time climbing up the ladder of power in the Planet, you could have been the Prime Minister in a few years. With wealth and power, you could have had your pick of all the women in the world. Why did you have to fixate on my sister? You have no vision. Instead, you stayed stuck where you were, in the Genesis Department, satisfied to help find a method to reduce our population!" The words spilled out from the Queen Immortal's mouth in quick succession.

"But contraception is of no use! The inferior people of Earth have nothing to do with their spare time, and are ruled by their carnal lust. We need revolutionary ideas for dealing with these stupid, sad lives. People who were born with nothing aspire to nothing. They shouldn't burden our resources with their sorry existence! And you can see the great results of my intervention. Within twenty years of your disappearance and my becoming the Genesis Director, I've designed a perfect world according to the heritage of people, with perfect class order and effective regulations. Low lives and people from the Merchant Class and below should not bear children. Some simple legislation and vigorous policing sufficed to cause our population to reduce itself by 37.8%! And Planet Earth has me to thank. It was only fitting for me to succeed Queen Thorpe when she passed away. In the past two years, since I become the Queen Immortal, I've weeded out many of the dissident Gentry and Nobles, too. They were too pliable, always feeling sorry for the lower classes. Well, I took care of that. They were all sent away to camps on other planets. Anyone who disobeys me and upsets my grand scheme for Earth deserves to be removed!"

Although Elizabeth had read about the atrocities of the Queen Immortal, she still found it hard to believe that the former Lady Catherine de Bourgh really thought she was doing the world a favour by enforcing her totalitarian rules and oppressive treatment of people. Elizabeth pressed her hands to her abdomen, hoping that Logan was sleeping and had not heard this tyrannical outburst.

But her hope was a vain one. *This woman is the Queen of La-la-land,* Logan told his mother. *Can we go out for some ice-cream instead of listening to her rubbish?*

"You're totally deranged!" Sir Lewis retorted. "People are born equal, and should be given equal rights and the freedom to choose whether they want children."

"Freedom and equality are just mirages! Such high ideals were invented by impractical philosophers who didn't live in the real world. Have you learned nothing from Earth's history? Behind almost every great advocate of freedom, liberty and equality, there has been a machine that used secrecy to mask self-gain. I, at least, am open about my actions, and I genuinely work for the good of the world! I've not taken one cent from the government since I ascended to the throne."

"But how many people have you killed because they disagreed with you or didn't follow your demented legislations?"

"I do not have to account to you for my actions. You no longer work for the government, by default since your disappearance. I am the Queen of this Planet, recognised by the United Galaxy Commission, and I now demand to be released! Darcy, you are ordered to untie me, this instant!"

Darcy looked at Elizabeth. She bit her lip. They did not have any legitimate reason to hold Queen Immortal here in the medical room, now that she had awakened and denied any involvement with Sir Lewis's disappearance or Queen Thorpe's death. And she could have had nothing to do with the detention of the Bennets, as she had been in a coma the entire time.

"A great deal has happened during your coma," Darcy said. "A Resistant Alliance was formed and has taken over the palace. Citizens have been rallying around the world, demanding a new government. UGC's representatives and hundreds of delegates from other planets are here, as well. We're going to discuss that new government in a few hours' time. I'll release you now, but your status is bound to be challenged, especially as the official seal is missing."

Her face grew red with fury. "I am the rightful ruler on Earth. I'm sure UGC will endorse the continuation of my power, with or without the seal. Bring Wickham to me! He will tell me where the seal is. He must have been keeping it in a safe place, waiting for my health to return."

"If you are the Queen," Sir Lewis said, "then I am the King. If I lost my job by default because of my disappearance, you lost yours by default through your loss of consciousness. Or perhaps you faked your own coma."

She glared at him. "You stupid, crazy man. I am going to tie you up, skin you alive and kill you, just as soon as I'm free. Your whole goal in life seems to be to make my life a misery."

Does the sedative have no effect anymore? Elizabeth wondered. *Why is Queen Immortal still so very ferocious?*

"Darcy, you no longer have to release Mrs. Catherine de Bourgh," Sir Lewis said. "She has threatened to harm me, in front of witnesses. I choose to press charges against her, because of these threats!" He patted Elizabeth's belly and whispered to her, "Logan is a genius! He has reminded me of how best to taunt my dear wife so that we can keep her locked up."

Elizabeth's eyes widened, not knowing what to do with her unborn son. Darcy, however, agreed with his uncle.

"Sorry, Aunt. I can't release you now, as you have declared yourself to be a danger to Sir Lewis. Until the matter of our ruler is resolved and your status becomes clearer, you must remain in restraints. But I will let you participate in the meeting with the UGC. I'll ask some officers from the RA to help you into a sitting position, but with the restraints still on."

The Queen burst into a torrent of abuse at her husband, nephew and anyone else she could think of. Elizabeth didn't want Logan to listen to more of the horrid words, and left the room, with a cheerful Sir Lewis following her. Darcy sent for an officer to guard the queen, then collected medical supplies and equipment and went to check on his wife.

After Sir Lewis left them in search of Anne and Georgiana, Elizabeth went to a guest room to rest.

"Your wound is closed properly," Darcy said, smoothing his knuckles over Elizabeth's shoulder after he checked on her.

"And Logan?"

I'm good, now that I'm away from my crazy great-aunt, the unborn Darcy replied.

"I'm talking to your father," Elizabeth chastised Logan.

"His vitals are all good," Darcy said. "But his mental development has increased tremendously again. The computer estimates that his brain function is almost that of a 10-year-old."

"My goodness! Will I be able to deliver him normally?"

"His physical size hasn't increased much since we last checked on him. Still on par with normal."

Stop worrying, Mom! We'll have the best doctors to take care of us.

Darcy embraced Elizabeth, caressing her back and abdomen. "Yes, Logan is right. I'll make sure the doctors provide you two with the best of care."

He gave her a reassuring kiss, touching her lips lightly, but she felt an urgent need to cleanse herself of the hatred that had radiated from the Queen Immortal's words. Grabbing his shoulders, she started to nibble his lips passionately.

The temperature soared in their bodies as their tongues duelled amorously. She dug her fingers over his back as he rubbed her butt in earnest. When they stopped to gasp for air, they gazed at each other with an intensity that symbolised eternal love.

"No regrets?" Elizabeth whispered.

"Definitely not," Darcy replied decidedly as he swept some wayward curls back from her face. "I meant every word I said to my aunt. You make me treat everyone as equal, and think about others first, before myself. You make me a better man, Elizabeth. I love you."

She gave him a smile and whispered, "I love you, too." Then she laid her head on his shoulders.

They embraced each other tightly for a long while before she drew them back to reality. "So, do you think your aunt really had nothing to do with Sir Lewis's exile on Hartfield?"

"She has no reason to deny it..."

She's lying, Logan said, jumping into the conversation between his parents.

"Why do you think so, Logan?" Darcy asked, frowning.

Her heartbeat was very irregular when she declared that she didn't make great uncle disappear, Logan explained. *It was the same when she said what she did about the other Queen's death. But I don't think she faked her own coma.*

"You can monitor heartbeats now?" Elizabeth rolled her eyes. There seemed to be no limits to baby Logan's ability.

I'm inside your womb, so everything's all dark. There's nothing better to do than listen to sounds, all kinds of them.

"Assuming Logan is correct," Darcy said, "that would mean that my aunt masterminded the removal of Uncle Lewis. But how can we prove that?"

Elizabeth replied, "She must have involved someone to transport Sir Lewis out of the Earth. If she hasn't gotten rid of them yet, we should be able to find some clues. Let's check the palace computer system for any encrypted files. We have a bit of time before the UGC meeting."

Yay! I second that, Logan added cheerfully. *It beats listening to you two kissing and saying cheesy stuff.*

"Logan!" Darcy said angrily.

"Logan, no ice cream for you!" Elizabeth said, and then turned to her husband. "I dread the day he begins talking like a teenager…"

Mom….Mommy….please…! Logan wailed.

Ignoring Logan's tantrum, Elizabeth shook her head and checked on the computers.

Voting Options

1) *General Fitzwilliam arrives in Hartfield*

2) **Sir Lewis's disappearance is explained** √

3) *United Galaxy Commission meeting*

CHAPTER FOURTEEN

A few hours later, the ballroom-turned-television-studio was transformed into a grand meeting room. Dignitaries from important planets, representatives from the United Galaxy Commission, and observers from major countries on Earth assembled. On the banks of monitors, citizens could be seen waiting eagerly on the streets. General Fitzwilliam, aboard his spaceship, was also asked to join in.

"I demand to be released this instant!" the Queen Immortal yelled. She was still in the medical room, but sitting on a chair, bound by restraints. Her image beamed into the grand ballroom.

"Go to hell, wax face!" a citizen on one of the monitors cried out.

"Quiet!" the General said. "Officer Morgan and crew, please make sure that the microphone is only turned on when the chairperson gives the signal for someone to speak."

The officers in the ballroom, and at every location where the televised meeting was being broadcast, acknowledged the instruction.

"Welcome to United Galaxy Commission meeting ZQXVI, held on 1540.43 at the floating palace on Planet Earth. I am

Catherine Moreland, the chairperson nominated to preside over this meeting. The proposed agenda for the meeting includes 1) The rule of George Wickham; 2) The military action of Planet Earth over Planet Hartfield and 3) In the absence of the official seal, the temporary governing arrangement on Earth

"This agenda was drawn up before Queen Catherine de Bourgh regained consciousness. Do any of you wish to propose additions to the agenda?" Moreland looked at the people seated around the table. They consisted of some of the representatives of the one hundred and thirty planets who could make the journey, and many non-voting but important members of those and other planets.

"General Fitzwilliam, do you have any additions?" Moreland asked Richard over the computer.

"Affirmative, Commissioner. I would like to add an item regarding the death of Queen Thorpe. I have new information that proves that her death and the disappearance of Sir Lewis are suspicious and related."

Disbelief adorned the faces of people around the world.

Moreland went around the panel, and the motion to add that new item to the agenda was accepted unanimously.

"As the legitimate ruler on Earth, Queen Catherine should have been asked to serve on the panel. But Sir Lewis, the previous Director of Genesis, husband to the Queen, who disappeared some twenty years ago, is pressing charges against the Queen for threats she made. The incident was witnessed and confirmed by Mr. Darcy of Pemberley. As a trial needs to be arranged, does anyone propose postponing this meeting until Queen Catherine can be on the panel?" Moreland continued.

"That could take months, and Planet Earth can't be left without a ruler in the meantime," Commander Frederick Wentworth commented. "Therefore, I propose that the meeting continue, with the chair being allowed discretion regarding Queen Catherine's participation in these proceeding."

"It's Earth's affair. We should not put our foot in it," said Prime Minister Willoughby from Planet Allenham. "I propose that we postpone the meeting and allow Queen Catherine to resume her rule immediately, until such time as she' is proven guilty."

"Is there a second for Commander Wentworth's proposal?" Moreland asked.

"I second," the newly promoted Commander Knightley said.

"And who seconds Prime Minister Willoughby's proposal?" Moreland asked.

"I do," Philip Elton of Highbury replied.

Moreland continued, "Before we put these proposals to a vote, Queen Catherine, do you have any statement to make?"

"I demand to be released this instant, you silly young girl! I was selected the rightful ruler by Earth's citizens two years ago. The election was confirmed by the United Galaxy Commission. This ridiculous allegation of threats was made up by my husband, who has gone mad after twenty years of imprisonment on Planet Hartfield. I should be allowed to rule until the official seal is found. UGC has no right to determine the fate of Planet Earth. I will respond to UGC about the military action regarding Planet Hartfield once I have resumed my rule."

Moreland's lips thinned, upon hearing Queen Immortal's disrespectful words. "The meeting was requested by a majority of the citizens of Earth, during your coma. It was deemed legitimate. The legal proceeding requested by Sir Lewis was also confirmed by Mr. Darcy of Pemberley. Mr. Darcy, do you have any concerns regarding the sanity of Sir Lewis?"

"Sir Lewis experienced temporary loss of memory during our stay on Planet Hartfield. Since his return to Earth, however, he has been under treatment and has regained a majority of his memory. I do not have any current concerns regarding his sanity, and I can confirm Queen Catherine's threats to him in the medical room."

"Darcy is mind-controlled by the whore beside him! She – " Queen Catherine's outburst was cut short by the sound engineer.

"Queen Catherine, I caution you to remain civilised during this meeting," Moreland said tightly, "to myself and to everyone else who is present. If there is another outburst, I will remove you from participation."

Queen Immortal opened her mouth, and her expression indicated that the next words she spoke were abusive, but the sound engineer did not bother to turn her microphone on.

"We shall now vote on Proposal One: to continue the meeting," Moreland announced. The votes were counted. "89 of the 123 votes in favour. Now for Proposal Two: to postpone the meeting….34 votes in favour. Proposal One carries. The United Galaxy Commission will proceed to discuss the agenda of the meeting, with discretionary participation from the former Queen Catherine on Earth. First item on the agenda: the rule of George Wickham on Earth. Lady Catherine de Bourgh, did you delegate the rule of Planet Earth to George Wickham under any circumstances?"

The former queen scowled at Moreland. "No, I did not. However, I..." The sound engineer cut the rest of her sentence off.

But the Prime Minister Willoughby jumped in. "No, no, let the grand lady continue. The committee would like to hear more about the circumstances."

"I did give him the official seal when I went into training of the andudas."

"I don't see an official announcement of the delegation of the seal, or a list of authorities to be temporarily relegated," Commander Wentworth said, scrolling through the computer database.

"It was of a peculiar nature," Lady Catherine replied, appearing flustered. "It was only for two weeks, so that he could oversee the retrieval of my nephew from rebellious Hartfield. I had no time for filling out the formalities."

"Nevertheless, according to Section 7, Regulation 129, any delegation of ruling power and official seal must be filed with the United Galaxy Commission within seven working days of its commencement." Moreland stared at the former Queen. "UGC thus deems this illegal, and declares the subsequent acts and administration by George Wickham to be void."

"I move that all prisoners captured during Wickham's time as Prince be released," Wentworth suggested. The motion carried, evoking jubilation in many areas on Earth.

"General Fitzwilliam, in the absence of a higher commanding officer in the army, the United Galaxy Commission now grants you authority to supervise the release of prisoners and oversee their compensation." Moreland made a notation on her computer console. "Now, moving on to the second item on the agenda, the military action of Planet Earth against Hartfield. Lady Catherine de Bourgh, what is your reply?"

"I don't have to explain myself to you, young girl! I authorised the deployment of the warships for a rescue mission, in light of the capture of Fitzwilliam Darcy of Pemberley. As he was a close relative of mine, I see Planet Hartfield's action as being in contravention of Article 13 of the Galactic Harmony Act."

Moreland ignored her. "Commander Knighley, what is Planet Hartfield's response?"

"I draw the attention of the United Galaxy Commission to Exhibit 1.0. Our planet has no record of any capture of Mr. Darcy prior to the entrance of three warships into our atmosphere. In addition, there was no UGC resolution, nor was there any warning prior to the attack. We did record two Earth beings aboard a Love Your Mate capsule which had been shot down by Planet Earth's Military Intelligence Agency in the previous hour. The male occupant did not identify himself with his full name. We did, however, ascertain that the male was Mr. Darcy at 138940 on the day of the attack, about 15 minutes prior."

"Documentation is verified accurate," Moreland said. "Lady Catherine, your response?"

"I only authorised the deployment of the warship for rescue, not to attack. Ask Commander Collins. Where is he, anyway?"

"Commander Collins is reported to have been killed in the air strike on Planet Hartfield," General Fitzwilliam stated. "An autopsy report of the Commander's body was ordered by George Wickham during his illegal rule. Here it is, submitted as Exhibit 2.0."

"Have any of the messages between the former Queen and his Commander survived, either on Earth or on the three warships?" Commander Wentworth questioned.

"Negative," General Fitzwilliam replied. "They conducted their communications on secret channels."

"In view of the absence of confirmed authorization regarding the attack by the former Queen of Earth, the United Galaxy Commission rules that the military action was illegally enacted by Commander Collins. However, as Planet Hartfield suffered material damages and human loss as a result of the illegal actions of one of Earth's military officers, I hereby recommend compensation, the extent of which shall be determined after Hartfield submits the full details of their losses. Are there any additional recommendations?"

Knightley replied in the negative, on behalf of his planet, though citizens on Earth were bemoaning yet another compensation to be forked out.

"No, good. Let's vote on it," Moreland continued.

The resolution passed easily.

"Now, regarding the third item on the agenda, concerning the death of Queen Thorpe and the disappearance of Sir Lewis, what do you have to report, General Fitzwilliam?"

"I would like to bring forward witness C Denny from Political Reality."

"What is the business of this witness?" Ambassador Moreland questioned.

"Mr. Denny has been a close friend of George Wickham's for many years. Upon the fall of the illegal Prince, the journalist was seen leaving Planet Earth with a suspicious amount of luggage, and was therefore searched, for security reasons. His personal belongings included such illicit items as drugs and weapons. While the discovery of these items would certainly be enough to send Mr. Denny to prison, it was the accidental recovery of several encrypted computer files within a pair of earrings in his possession that shed new light upon the disappearance of Sir Lewis, some twenty years ago, and the death of Queen Thorpe, two years earlier."

"Permission to bring forward C Denny is granted."

After the oath, Denny took his place on the witness stand.

"Who does this pair of earrings belong to?" Moreland asked.

"George Wickham," Denny replied.

"How did they come to be in your possession?"

"Well, I heard George – I mean, Wickham – had been changed. I mean, turned into a woman. They said he couldn't remember a thing. So I thought it would do no harm to take a few of his things to sell. He owes me over 9,000 quid from past years. The earrings have some small diamonds in them. I hoped they would be enough."

"Were you aware of the encrypted files hidden inside?"

"Absolutely not. I'm not that good with computers, anyway."

"Have you ever seen George Wickham wearing them?"

"Yes, regularly, after he was promoted as Tea-Leaf Reader."

"Are you currently aware of the information contained in those encrypted files?"

"No, Madam."

"You may step down now. General Fitzwilliam, please proceed with a brief summary of the information recovered."

"Yes, Ambassador Moreland. The encrypted files are submitted as Exhibit 3.0. I would like to broadcast an extracted conversation from the files, to facilitate the UGC's understanding."

"Proceed."

General Fitzwilliam signalled to his staff, and a conversation began to broadcast. Queen Thorpe was lying on her bed, one hand clutching her throat in pain.

"What did you put in the wine?" the dying Queen said.

Someone not within the view of the camera said, in a digitised, mechanical male voice, "Some happy stuff." He laughed. "To make you go away."

"Like what you did with Lewis?" She tried to grab her tormentor, but the latter moved away.

"I'm being kinder to you," he snorted. "I dropped Lewis down a hell hole in Hartfield. He's still suffering, I'm sure. But you, you'll have no worries anymore."

"Why?" Queen Thorpe twisted in bed, in spasms. "I hid your secret. I've been so good to you. And this is your repayment of my kindness?"

"Kindness doesn't make greatness." His laughter was full of smugness. "I want to be the Greatest! Family and friends in my way have to be gone."

The footage went black as the eerie laugh of the killer echoed in the ears of everyone present. Many looked at Queen Immortal with suspicious eyes, while the former Queen sat on her chair, expressionless.

Ambassador Moreland drew a deep breath and took over the meeting again.

"General, are you able to identify the sound of the murderer?"

"Not yet, Ambassador. We're working on it."

"And other information from the files?"

"It included a log of the journey someone took to Hartfield on a secret cruiser, to dispose of Sir Lewis, as well as a record of a cash transaction paid to Queen Thorpe, probably for keeping the secret."

"The killer has been paying Queen Thorpe for twenty years. He must be very wealthy," Commander Wentworth commented, eyeing the former Queen in the medical room with keen interest.

"This is an internal affair involving Planet Earth. The United Galaxy Commission will leave it in your hands, General Fitzwilliam, with the request that we be informed once the murderer is identified," Moreland said. "We will now proceed to the next item on today's agenda, regarding the official seal for Planet Earth. What progress have you to report, General?"

"Originally Wickham alleged that the seal had been sent to Hartfield. I was halfway there when I discovered otherwise."

"Where is it, then? Are your men close to its recovery?"

"Not yet. However, according to our computer records, no vessel, official or commercial, has left Earth for Hartfield in the timeframe during which Wickham was in possession of the seal. The three warships that attacked Harfield, under the command of Collins, were recruited from other locations. We have also ascertained that no beaming has been performed within that time frame. We can only conclude, therefore, that the seal is still on Earth. Wickham, with his memory corrupted due to a botched medical procedure, is assisting as best he can with the search. However, it may be some time before we can locate the official seal."

Moreland nodded. "Are there any additional comments regarding the recovery of the official seal?"

Lady Catherine had been hurling a string of words throughout General Fitzwilliam's answer. Moreland waved permission for her voice to be heard.

"...even without the bloody seal, I'm still the rightful ruler on Earth! It's thanks to me that the Earth's population growth has been controlled. Otherwise, all these bloody savages would just produce and produce...."

Moreland had heard enough, and waved for amplification of her voice to be turned off. "In light of the missing seal," she said, "does anyone have a resolution for the temporary rule on Planet Earth?"

"I nominate Elizabeth Bennet as temporary ruler on Earth, until the next general election in one and a half year's time, even if the seal is recovered in interim," Commander Wentworth said.

"I nominate that rule be divided between the members of a United Galaxy Commission committee," Prime Minister Willoughby of Planet Allenham said, "said committee to be headed by representatives of two of the nearest planets."

Reaction from the citizens on Earth was mixed. Many had come to think of Elizabeth as a symbol of their fight against the autocratic rule of Queen Immortal. But her association with the rich and powerful Mr. Darcy made people wary of her. While Willoughby was handsome, and his proposal seemed objective, Earth's citizens didn't want to be ruled by a bunch of foreigners. And the last suggestion made by Willoughby wasn't entirely impartial. Allenham was the nearest planet. He wanted a piece of Earth's rule!

Voting Options

1) *Lizzy declines the presidency*

2) **Lizzy accepts the presidency** √

3) *A referendum is held to elect the president*

CHAPTER FIFTEEN

Commissioner Moreland asked the floor, "Is there any other proposal waiting to be heard regarding the temporary rule on Planet Earth?"

"I propose that Planet Earth expedite the hearing of Queen Catherine's case within the next two weeks. Should she be found not guilty of the charges made against her by Sir Lewis, she should then be returned as the rightful ruler," Mr. Elton said.

On hearing this proposal, many people around the globe grew agitated. They shouted their dislike of the possibility of having the autocratic queen return. Although their voices were not transmitted into the meeting room, the delegates could see their angry faces and their makeshift banners that spelled out their discontent.

Moreland continued, "The next general election on Earth is slated for the middle of 3820, in one and a half year's time. Before we put the three proposals to vote by citizens on Earth, the Commission would like to ask the main candidates concerned to speak before the Commission. The two nearest planets to Earth are Allenham and Kellynuch. Prime Minister Willoughby, Sir Walter Elliot and Mrs. Elizabeth Darcy, we will adjourn the meeting for an hour, after which we expect to hear from you about your decision and plan."

Elizabeth went into one of the conference rooms and requested the presence of her husband, her father, Jane and Mr. Bingley. General Fitzwilliam joined them online, as well.

"I want to decline the offer," Elizabeth declared.

"It's more trouble than it's worth, my dear," Mr. Bennet said. "I agree with your decision."

"I don't trust Willoughby to surrender rule after the election." Richard scowled. "In fact, I doubt he would hold the election at all!"

"He seems a charming man," Jane said. "Surely the United Galaxy Commission would not allow that to happen."

"UGC has a surfeit of bureaucracy, and mounds of tedious rules and regulations. Once we install foreign people on Earth, it may take a while to get rid of them," Darcy commented.

"I hate to say so, but I agree with Darcy," Bingley added.

"I don't have the experience and skill to manage a planet." Elizabeth frowned. "And I will be giving birth in a few months' time. Logan is my first priority. I could not devote all of my energy to the administration."

"Yes, and I won't have her overtire herself, either," Darcy affirmed, and nodded. "There is no way I want her away from me." He put his arm around her shoulders.

"We could easily solve that by stationing the floating palace at Pemberley," Richard suggested. "And we could recommend advisers to help you."

"Why do you want my Lizzy to take up this troublesome presidency?" Mr. Bennet asked.

"I have heard many unsavoury rumours about Willoughby and Sir Walter," the General said.

"Such as?"

"Willoughby seduced several female staff in the Prime Minister's Office, and has used Government money to host extravagant parties."

"Then why has his behaviour not been exposed?" Elizabeth demanded. "How many women are we talking about?"

"He has the Government money and connections to keep all his young girls happy in Allenham. The documents I discovered estimated that there were about six of them."

Jane gasped.

He's a really bad guy! Logon commented to his mother. *You can't let him rule on Earth.*

"And it's not just about his indiscretions," Richard continued. "He has been leading Sir Walter into some very expensive pursuits, too."

"What sort of pursuits?" Bingley questioned.

"Sir Walter has purchased two of the latest-model B98 happy-gas warships, on Willoughby's recommendation. He is using one to scout what he calls 'unsettled territory' on Planet Kellynuch. He wants to develop and raise flying horses. But those lands belong to native tribes of Kellynuch. I've already heard about some fighting going on in those areas. He deploys a heavily equipped army, while the natives use primitive weapons. I fear he would want Planet Earth for housing his captives or expanding his pleasure grounds."

"And the other warship?" Darcy asked. "What happened to it?"

"He lent it to Willoughby. I'm not sure what Willoughby wants it for, unless he's interested in attacking neighbouring planets."

"Why is UGC not doing anything?" Elizabeth said.

"Because they have covered their tracks very well. I only know about it because of the secret dossiers I found while searching Aunt Catherine's personal computer."

"Then we cannot have these men ruling Planet Earth, no matter for how short a period!" Bingley exclaimed.

"Can you show me the evidence?" Elizabeth asked.

General Fitzwilliam proceeded to display the secret dossiers.

"What do you intend to do with this evidence?" Darcy asked, seeing that the information was extremely comprehensive.

"I'm going to hand it over to a trusted friend in UGC. We don't want Willoughby and Sir Walter to know we've exposed them. It could cause interplanetary incidents. Although the evidence was quite extensive, some of its authenticity may be debated."

"Now that we know of Willoughby and Sir Walter's ambition, I cannot let them have their way." Elizabeth said. "But I'm still not convinced that I am the right person for the job. Who are the advisors you have in mind, Richard?"

"How about you, Bingley?" General Fitzwilliam said.

Bingley shook his head and replied, "Thank you for the confidence, Richard. But, as Mr. Bennet has pointed out, Jane and I are so compliant that nothing would ever be resolved; so easy, that every staff member would cheat us; and so generous, that we will always exceed our income. I wouldn't want my indecision to hurt the Earth or deplete our Planet's treasury."

"And Darcy isn't suitable," Richard added.

"Yes, his familial association with Queen Catherine is most unfortunate," Bingley nodded. "The same applies to you, Richard."

"Then we must look outside of our circle to find someone to support Elizabeth," Darcy said.

"What do you know about Commander Wentworth and Ambassador Moreland?" Elizabeth asked.

"Commander Wentworth has had a highly decorated exploration career for this planet. He has undertaken many successful rescue and discovery missions. He's recently married to Anne Elliot, his childhood sweetheart, after seven years of separation. I think he has great analytical skill and an eye for detail, although I am less clear about his leadership skills. And because of his work, he's away too often. I was actually thinking of Commander Brandon of Delaford."

"He's not a member of the United Galaxy Commission," Bingley said.

"No, but he knows Willoughby very well. I believe they have a history. And I've known Brandon for many years. He's fair, honourable and diligent. I think, if he agrees, that he will be well able to defend our interests."

"He sounds like you," Elizabeth said to her husband.

"I'm handsomer," Darcy whispered.

She arched her brows and turned to question the General. "And Catherine Moreland?"

"Moreland would be a good complement on the team. She is rather young, but her people skills and diplomatic abilities are well known. She's become quite the favourite commissioner in the UGC, heading a few missions that required good negotiation techniques. That's why she was selected to chair today's meeting."

"But would it work, having two foreigners assist Lizzy? Would they help her workload?" Darcy asked.

"They would just be advisors to help Elizabeth with important decisions. The government is run by the ministers anyway. Elizabeth, you probably will mostly be busy reviewing and amending the restrictive and autocratic rules imposed by Lady Catherine and Wickham over these past years," General Fitzwilliam added in summation.

After the discussion, the others left the Darcys to discuss the matter amongst themselves.

"What do you truly think, Fitzwilliam?"

"I'm worried about Logan." He placed his hand on Elizabeth's belly.

Hey, Dad, you don't need to be a worry wart! I'm a big boy. I eat and sleep well. I can even help Mom with her paperwork.

"Why are you so keen on your mom becoming the president? Is it vanity?"

I feel a bad vibe from that Willoughby. And, of course, my great-aunt and former queen is rather crazy. Who's better suited to keep everyone on Earth safe than my wonderful mother? You wouldn't have married her if she wasn't smart and marvellous, Dad!

Darcy rolled his eyes again. "There is no arguing with Logan. He's way too smart for his age."

"Well, I must admit that I don't feel happy about the prospect of leaving the rule to Willoughby or Sir Walter, either," Elizabeth said. "We have had two horrendous years, suffering from the Queen Immortal and Prince Wickham. If those in charge decide to skim our citizens for even more money, or institute even stricter regulations, we'll suffer again."

Darcy nodded.

She sighed. "I think I'm inclined to accept the position now, for the next year and a half, should I be elected. We can encourage more candidates to come forward for the presidential election then."

Yea! Logan cheered. *Mother President! President Mrs. Darcy!*

"I'll support whatever decision you make," Darcy pledged. "As Richard suggested, we can park the palace at Pemberley, and you won't have to travel far to go to work. Everyone in Pemberley will see to your needs." He lowered his head and gave her a reassuring kiss.

With this new-forged agreement, the Darcys returned to the grand meeting room.

Sir Walter was the first to speak. "Citizens of Earth, I would be honoured to work with Prime Minister John Willoughby of Allenham to ensure that happiness and freedom are restored on Earth. After years of your ruler's suppression, I propose to allow total freedom for all people. You will be free to have sex, choose your partners and marry whomever you want, once we are elected. Indeed, you can have as many babies as you wish, with whomever you wish – even the aliens. Haha! There will be more pleasure facilities built for you in the next years. Life is short, so play as hard as you can. Now, Willoughby, charm their socks off," Sir Walter concluded.

"Thank you, Sir Walter, and thank you, Citizens of Earth. I would be honoured to be allowed a chance to work for you. I am the youngest Prime Minister in Allenham, and therefore I understand the pain and suffering of the young people on Earth. The galaxy has been ruled by too many staid and boring old men and women for too long – Sir Walter excepted, as he is high on partnering with young people. You need a voice, and I will speak loudest for you. I'll cry, scream and yell for your welfare, until your desires are met. I'll be passionate, fervent and energetic in my work. You won't find my plans and recommendations boring or traditional. I'll push Earth to a new era, with new frontiers and experiences. Who do you want to speak for you, work for you and help you reach new heights? The crazy old Queen Immortal? Her rich nephew's unknown wife? Or a man with passion and vision?"

Willoughby then bowed deeply and left the floor for Elizabeth to speak.

"Dear fellow citizens, thank you for nominating me to become the temporary caretaker of Earth. I may not be as well known in the Galaxy as Sir Walter or Mr. Willoughby, but I know about your worries and issues, because I am one of you. My plans for the next year and a half would include, firstly, recruiting two advisers who have more experience in government and political decision-making than I, myself, possess, to help me navigate through these complex issues.

"Second, I would review and remove the unfair and autocratic laws imposed by the former Queen and George Wickham. Thirdly, I would identify suitable permanent presidential candidates to participate in the election in 3820. Fourth, I would work with inventors, scientists and agriculturalists to find solutions to the pressure on our food supply.

"Lastly, I recommend abolishing the class system that has been in place for so long. I believe in equality. A lord is born on Earth, of his loving parents. I am also born here, of my dear parents. We should be treated equally in our right to work, live, marry and have children. I promise that I will be fair, diligent and compassionate. And I hope to help our planet become a happier place for our children, from now on. Thank you."

Yea, Mom! I love your speech! Logan said. He was over-excited, and technicolour was visible on Elizabeth's belly.

Finally Moreland called on the Queen to give her speech.

"Poosh, poosh. All nonsense here! Walter is an overindulged fool. Willoughby is a scoundrel who uses government money to party and seduce girls. That tramp that Darcy married is a schemer. I am the rightful ruler on Earth. I have controlled our population. You all have what you need. Why would you want other people to rule over you? Without strict laws, the world will sink into anarchy. If you know what's good for you, you will vote to reinstall me as Queen Immortal!"

"Thank you," Moreland said. "We are now open for voting from around the world. Each city has two votes."

The procedure of voting was explained and then the process began.

After an hour, it was announced that Mrs. Elizabeth Darcy had been elected as the new president on Planet Earth, with a 69% majority. Willoughby and Sir Walter's partnership each won 25% of the vote, and a die-hard six percent had voted for the Queen Immortal.

Elizabeth's request for assistance from Ambassador Catherine Moreland and Commander Brandon was also accepted.

After the long day, the delegates left for their respective residences on Earth, or journeyed back to their home planets. The Darcys decided to stay for a few more days in the floating palace in London. They would travel on to Pemberley in a week's time.

When they returned to their sleeping quarters in the palace, they were met with chaotic yelling and screaming.

"What's happening?" Darcy asked with concern.

"It's Lydia!" Mrs. Bennet cried. "She's gone mad. She came from nowhere and tried to attack me. What has happened to my favourite girl? Who turned her into a killer? She didn't even recognise me!"

"Luckily there were some security guards protecting us," Kitty said. "But she wouldn't give up her weapon or surrender."

"Don't hurt my girl!" Mrs. Bennet yelled, as the guards tried to shoot at Lydia.

"She's been brainwashed. I don't think she can stop." Elizabeth tightened her hold on Darcy's hand.

Get Grand-Uncle Lewis! He could freeze her! Logan exclaimed.

"Oh, yes! Good thinking Logan. Guards, don't shoot her yet. Kitty, run along to the medical room and get Sir Lewis," Elizabeth patted her swollen belly and said, "He may be able to help."

During the ensuing five minutes of intense fighting between the security guards and Lydia, the Bennets and Darcys stood at the periphery and held their breath, worried that there would be a casualty.

Luckily, Sir Lewis soon arrived, with Georgiana in tow.

"What's happening here?" he asked.

"Please, Uncle," Darcy replied, "can you stop Elizabeth's younger sister? She's been brainwashed by George Wickham. She won't willingly stop until she has killed all of the Bennets and Darcys."

Sir Lewis pressed his lips thin. Focusing his eyes on Lydia, he raised his hand and waved at her. After several attempts, however, he realised that he couldn't freeze her action. "No, her mind has been tampered with."

Georgiana passed something to her brother. Darcy had a look and said, "Let me shoot her."

"No!" Mrs. Bennet screamed. "You can't kill my girl!"

"Of course not. I will use the tranquiliser."

"Double the dose," Sir Lewis suggested. "She won't be easily subdued."

Elizabeth handed Darcy the medicine, and he aimed at Lydia.

Pop!

Pop!

Pop!

It took three shots to subdue her. Lydia screamed when the shots pierced her shoulder. Her eyes went red, and she leaped away from the security guards and pounced toward Darcy. Before she could reach him, however, she was thrown backwards by Logan and Sir Lewis, working in tandem.

Finally, with a loud, pain-filled yell, Lydia twisted on the floor and then lay still.

"Guards, disarm her and take her to the medical room," Elizabeth directed.

The guards moved to kick Lydia's weapon away.

Cling!

Cling!

"What's the matter?" Elizabeth asked, as she saw the guards freeze.

One of them went towards the wall, where the schiavona sword had hit it.

"Madam, there's something hidden inside the hilt of her ancient sword," the guard said.

"What is it?"

He crouched down and looked up at her in surprise. "It's the seal!"

Voting Options

1) A secret is revealed √

2) Someone's future is decided

3) Someone is rescued

CHAPTER SIXTEEN

"Please conduct my sister to the medical room," Elizabeth instructed, taking the seal and Lydia's sword from the guard.

"I do hope she still has her memory," Mrs. Bennet cried. "What if she stays a robotic killer forever? How can she get married?"

"Mrs. Bennet, the Palace has an excellent medical team," Darcy said. "And my sister is well versed in computer programming. She may find out how to reverse the brainwashing function. We will help Lydia recover."

"Mom, let's go with her," Kitty urged.

Mrs. Bennet nodded. "Kitty and I will go to the medical room. Lizzy, tell your father to come at once. I need him to demand the best possible treatment for my Lydia."

"Yes, I'll locate Dad now," Elizabeth replied.

Once Mrs. Bennet and Kitty left the room, the Darcys took the seal back to the administration headquarters of the palace. Then Elizabeth sent out an alert for her father, who was soon located in the library of the Palace.

"Papa, Mom wants you to go to the medical room. We've found Lydia and subdued her. She's being treated there."

He stood immediately. "Is she harmed?"

"No, she's fine. But she didn't respond to us. We'll need to see if the doctors can reverse the brainwashing procedure and recover her memory. It may be best for you to see to her, though. The doctors may be seeking consents."

He nodded and hurried out of the library.

After that, Elizabeth called up the communication channel. "Let's alert Richard about the seal."

General Fitzwilliam soon came online.

"Ah, you've arrived at Hartfield," Darcy said, seeing the vision from Richard's cruiser.

"Yes," the general replied. "With Commander Knightley's escort, we arrived at 109062. They will direct us to the unsettled portion of the planet. But we don't know where Wickham's camp is, so it may take us some time to locate my parents and the other captives."

"We've just recovered the seal," Elizabeth said. "Perhaps it can help you find where the camp is."

"Marvellous! Where did you find it?"

"It was with my sister. Lydia had concealed it in her sword. What shall we do with the seal?" Elizabeth asked.

"Is it damaged?"

"No, it looks to be in good condition." Elizabeth stroked the diamond edges of the seal.

"You need to fit it into the lock on the vault."

"There is a vault here?" Darcy asked.

"Yes. It's used for storing confidential official documents and physical items that could be used to change or disarm passwords of the treasury account. Without the seal and a way to unlock the password, the government will run out of funds in thirty days. And I'm hoping Wickham has some secret files stored in the computer there that link to the files from the earrings, and can point to the locations where my parents are."

"Where is the vault?"

"In Underground Section 821 of the Palace. Be sure to bring Colonel Morgan and some guards with you when you go there."

"You're afraid Wickham may have set some booby traps in there?" Darcy asked.

"We mustn't underestimate his madness," the general replied. "Keep me posted on what you find. I will talk to Knightley and delay the journey for another eight hours."

Elizabeth summoned Colonel Morgan and a group of six heavily armed guards, and went with them to Section 821.

"Let me go before you," Darcy said protectively. Elizabeth nodded and allowed him to go ahead of her, just behind the guards.

To everyone's relief, the corridor was clear.

When they arrived at the door of the vault, Elizabeth stepped forward to unlock it with the seal, but Darcy advised against it.

"Mrs. President, allow me," Colonel Morgan said.

Nodding, Elizabeth handed him the seal.

With the help of the guards, they fit the seal to the lock, then used some extendable forceps to open it from a distance. The seal fitted and turned without a problem...

Click!

Clack!

Click!

...and the door of the vault opened!

After the guards made sure that there was no danger inside, Elizabeth and Darcy entered. It was a small room, roughly four meters square. One wall was taken up by functioning computers and monitors, while another contained physical objects fitted at different levels, a total of sixteen, in all.

Elizabeth sat down in front of the computers and began to check the files. She found that she could check the directories, but was unable to open any of the files.

"Should I check on the objects?" Darcy asked.

Elizabeth cautioned, "Yes, but make sure not to disrupt their present location, in case the level they are on has significance, as well."

Darcy nodded.

As Elizabeth worked on the computers silently, Darcy checked all of the objects with meticulous care. There were ancient objects, like a radio and a clock, as well as present-day items like a plasma hand.

"Hey, I think I may have found something!" Elizabeth exclaimed.

"What is it?" Darcy held onto the plasma hand and came to stand behind his wife.

"This file. It has a very strange property code. Nothing similar to those within this folder." She copied several codes from different files and tried to crack the password. "Umh, it's rather difficult. I will feed in an automatic decoding program and let it run while I try other files. I'll call Richard, too. Maybe the encrypted files from the earrings could unlock it."

Darcy didn't say anything, knowing that this was her specialty. Instead, he returned his attention to the plasma hand he was holding. It was a strange object, translucent. He could see all the electric nerves in it. But the nails were black, which didn't seem to be in harmony with the rest of the design or the texture of the plasma hand.

He was about to put it back in its place when a beam flashed from the computer and shone onto the black fingernail.

"What just happened?" Elizabeth asked in surprise, and turned to look at him.

The nail on the thumb changed colour, from black to grey and finally to transparent, similar to the nerves in the hand.

"I don't know." Darcy bit his lip and thought for a minute. "It looks as if the computer can activate some changes in this hand."

He brought it nearer to the computer and turned the hand at different angles.

The fingernails changed from black to crystal-clear, one by one. When the last colour change was complete, the fingers of the plasma hand closed together for a moment and then stretched wide, like opening the palm. The action stroked the screen of the computer, and one of the locked files opened up.

"I see. We have to match each file with an object!" Elizabeth exclaimed, surprised by how the password had been cracked, embedded in the nail of the plasma hand. "Interesting!"

"What does it store?"

"Let me see." Both of them looked at the letters and numbers on the screen. "Um, it seems to be text from an ancient document."

To disobey her mother by refusing an Unexceptionable offer is not enough; 23968; her affections must also be given without her mother's approbation; 76452. I never saw a girl of her age bid fairer to be the sport of mankind; 34501. Her feelings are tolerably acute; 84723, and she is so charmingly artless in their display as to afford the most reasonable hope of her being ridiculous, and despised by every man who sees her; 37251. Artlessness will never do in love matters; 84632;

and that girl is born a simpleton who has it either by nature or affectation.

"Umh, what does this mean?" Darcy stroked his jaw.

"It must contain some special codes. Let me feed several possibilities in." Elizabeth typed quickly. "The program can decipher the code, using different combination of logic."

"What do you think the computer file contains?"

Perhaps bad prince Wickham has channelled some money to his own bank account in another galaxy, Logan said.

"You could be right, son," Darcy replied. He massaged Elizabeth's shoulders. "Are you feeling all right? It's two in the morning already. What an eventful day! You're not too tired?"

"I'm fine," she replied. "I'm a night owl."

"I hope we find the murderer of Queen Thorpe soon. I can't rest until he's put away, especially now that you've become the temporary president. He may want to harm you." He kissed her forehead and gave her a hug while they waited for the program to work.

She rested her head on his chest. "I hope some information can help Richard locate his parents in time."

Beep!

Beep!

A string of characters emerged, after the program combined the letters and numbers in a different way.

"Brain," Elizabeth read it out as the word was formed. "Numbing...torpedo sprays...installed...in Hawaii...and Portugal...to control...population of...Northern... Hemisphere!"

"My god!" Darcy exclaimed.

"We need to find their locations at once!" Elizabeth cried out, busily typing again. As soon as the general came online, she said, "Richard, we found a secret file. There are brain-controlling torpedo sprays installed in facilities in Hawaii and

Portugal. Wickham wants to control the entire population of the Northern Hemisphere."

"Shit!" Richard exclaimed. "Are they time-activated? When will they blast off?"

"The program here is still deciphering the codes," Darcy explained.

"Mrs. President, please deploy all ground units to identify the torpedoes and destroy them," the general requested formally.

"I will summon Moreland and Brandon to support the decree this minute," Elizabeth assured him.

The whole approval was completed in less than fifteen minutes. By that time, the program had disclosed more information. Unfortunately, the location of the torpedoes was not included, but a document revealed that they would blast off at the time scheduled for the planned execution of the Bennets, presumably because the wicked prince believed he could distract the world with that televised event, a grim deadline that was only twenty hours away.

As Mrs. President Darcy, her advisors and the general busily coordinated the deployment of the troops, Darcy, who had taken over keeping track of the decoding of the secret files, called out, "Here is the murderer's bank account!"

Elizabeth looked over his shoulders. "Where is it being held?"

"At Galaxy Haven."

Elizabeth scanned the information on the screen. "A million a year, at first, and then it progressed to three million each year, for the past twenty years! Who would have such wealth?"

"It's Aunt Catherine!" Darcy said, his voice tight with anger.

Yeah, I told you she was lying. Logan jumped, projecting technicolour from Elizabeth's belly.

"But it's strange," Darcy murmured. "The writing and signature are different, from what I've known as Aunt's."

"Let's examine some official documents," Elizabeth said. With a few keystrokes, she called up a variety of handwritten documents by the Queen from throughout the years.

"Hmm. In the official documents, they all look similar." Darcy frowned. "Nothing like these strange ones here."

"Can we get a copy of the original record from Haven?" Elizabeth asked. "Was there a fingerprint or photo ID?"

"We can probably go through the United Galaxy Commission for an inter-galaxy matter," Darcy suggested.

"I'll do that. And I have to put your aunt under arrest."

Darcy nodded, his face grim.

"There is still more information coming out. You should continue to see if there is any mention of the torpedo sprays." Elizabeth smoothed her hands on his arms, knowing that it was hard for him to know that his close relative was cold enough to have sent her husband to suffer for twenty years. He must have hoped that his Aunt Catherine was not involved. But it seemed the old woman's resentment over Darcy's mother was so great that she had had no scruples about doing it.

Another hour passed, and the file data ended without revealing any other important information.

"Is there any other similar file with odd structure?" Darcy asked.

Elizabeth stopped her communication with Moreland and Brandon and typed in a few other formulae to check for abnormality.

Not much later, she found what she sought. "This file looks irregular. Do you think we need another object from the wall to unlock the password?" Elizabeth murmured.

"I'll look at them," Darcy said.

He went through the remaining items again: fashionable hat, a pointed shoe, a miniature crocodile. Nothing seemed to be useful as an object for unlocking the password.

While Elizabeth continued to run programs and link the files from the earrings to try to crack the password of the file, Commander Brandon had been working on the ground with the national armies to scout various areas in Portugal and Hawaii.

"We need to approach the whole thing from a different angle," Elizabeth said at last, brushing the loose locks from her forehead. Tired and frustrated, she asked, "Do we know how large this kind of torpedo spray will be?"

Moreland and the general, on the other end of the communication network, considered her question. "There are many designs throughout the years. A large one can be as large as a hand-held rocket. But a small one could be as little as a grenade."

"If Wickham went for the smaller versions and installed many of them, we won't be able to remove all of them in time." Elizabeth murmured.

"Unfortunately, that is true," Moreland and General Fitzwilliam agreed.

"Do you think he entrusted them to his followers? Perhaps he had them install the sprays in secret locations," Darcy speculated.

"I have an idea," Elizabeth said. "But I am going to cross-match those who just voted for the Queen Immortal to be reinstalled with their place of residence, and see if many of them live in Portugal and Hawaii. If so, we can search their premises, as a precautionary measure."

"That's a good idea!" the general agreed.

"Can we also do one more thing?" Darcy asked, pacing.

"What idea do you have?" Richard said.

"To use the same tactic as Wickham used."

"What do you mean, Mr. Darcy?" Moreland asked.

"Can we direct a televised address to people in those areas, saying that Wickham has given them up, and that those who do not surrender the weapons they have will be rounded up and sent to prison?"

"But that might cause widespread panic." Elizabeth thought for a second. "I have another idea. We could have someone impersonate Wickham, and have him appeal to his followers to give up their weapons. He could claim that he has asked for a pardon from the temporary government, and that he needs the co-operation of his followers in order for the pardon to succeed."

"The strategy can back-fire," Darcy said.

"Why?" Elizabeth asked.

"When people see the televised message, they will expect the new government to actually pardon him. We can't do that if his weapons kill many people. And the same panic situation might result."

"So the best way is still for us to find the weapons. I had better crack the codes in time," Elizabeth said grimly, and continued to work on the computer, as another software engineer was brought in to assist her.

Unfortunately, four hours before the scheduled time of blastoff, they still hadn't broken the codes, and so Elizabeth decided to try the risky strategy, after consulting with her advisers.

They went to the medical room, where Elizabeth pulled Georgiana and the doctors aside and told them about the situation.

"We're still trying to reactivate Wickham's previous memory, before it was accidentally mixed with Caroline's," Georgiana said. She took the Darcys to the room where Wickham was. He was conscious, with many wires affixed to his head, and his eyes darted around strangely.

"Continue with your work," Elizabeth said. "I've brought some CGI graphic experts with me. They are going to scan Wickham and produce a life-sized likeness. We will then use it to speak our piece."

"My dear Mr. Darcy," Wickham called out. "Marry me!"

Darcy shivered at the sound of Wickham's sickeningly sweet and fawning voice, which sounded far too much like Caroline Bingley.

"Say yes, and I'll tell you whatever you want to know." Princess Wickham smiled coquettishly. His hands and legs were restrained, but he swayed his body, trying to thrust his well-endowed breasts seductively at Darcy.

"What can you tell me?" Darcy stepped backward and scowled, unsure whether the gender-changed psychotic in the bed knew what he was saying.

"I'll tell you where George has hidden the torpedo sprays," Wickham offered, talking about himself as if he was another person, "but only if you marry me in front of all the people of Earth, televised. I always wanted to marry in orange. I'll be much admired. The Royal Wedding of the century. The handsomest Mr. Darcy and the most elegant Caroline Bingley. Women will copy my hair style, my wedding dress, my..." He went on and on, speaking more like Caroline than Wickham.

Yuck! Demented George Wickham and Caroline Bingley, all in one! Logan exclaimed. *You can't marry my father. He is already married to Mother President! Stay away from him!*

Elizabeth patted her belly. She couldn't agree more with Logan, this time. Wickham/Caroline's mind was twisted. Twisted...

She suddenly had an idea.

Pulling Darcy out of the room, she said to him, "Fitzwilliam, I think you should marry Caroline/Wickham!"

Voting Options

1) A wedding is conducted

2) Someone is punished √

3) Someone is injured

CHAPTER SEVENTEEN

"What?" Darcy's widened at such an insane declaration.

How could you suggest that, Mom? Logan protested loudly to his mother. He must have kicked, as Elizabeth felt a sudden contraction. She gasped and held onto Darcy's arms.

"What is the matter?" Darcy asked anxiously.

"Logan is kicking too hard..." She drew in a deep breath.

I'm sorry, Mom! Logan said. *I didn't mean to hurt you. I just couldn't stand the thought of even a fake wedding between Dad and that awful man-turned-woman princess.*

Scowled, Darcy settled Elizabeth in the nearest chair, and caressed her belly and back tenderly. Then, with a stern voice, he talked to his unborn son. "Logan, if you ever do that again to your mother, I am going to put you on the timeout stool for a long time – once you're old enough to be put there!"

Logan replied in a quivering voice, *Yes, Dad! I promise. Mom, too. I swear. I love you both. I won't do anything to hurt either of you.*

Elizabeth nodded her head and pressed her hands on her belly. With a few more deep breaths, she felt the pain fading away.

"That was not acceptable, Logan," Darcy said sternly. "You must understand that I can't let it go without punishment."

Yes, Dad.

Darcy embraced Elizabeth and let her rest as he thought about a suitable reprisal. "For your punishment, son...you are not allowed to say anything for the next two days."

Oh...! That's bad... Yes, Dad, Mom, I am sorry.

Elizabeth patted her stomach. "Apology accepted. Now off you go."

Thanks, Mom, for not being angry with me, Logan said meekly, and subsided into silence.

Darcy sighed. "Elizabeth, I don't think that's a good idea for me to marry this Caroline-Wickham mixture. It would make me ill, just seeing him – I mean, her – in an orange wedding dress. And for him to cling to my arm as we say the vows... What if he demands consummation before he'll tell us anything?"

"But what are we going to do?" Elizabeth's voice filled with anguish. "It's only another three hours to the deadline! We can't let the people in Portugal and Hawaii be infected with that brain-numbing virus. They would become virtual zombies."

I agree with Dad! Mom, the bad prince only remembers haphazardly. What if Dad has the wedding with him, but then he can't remember anything about where he put all the torpedo sprays?

"Logan!" Both Darcy and Elizabeth exclaimed at their son, who clearly did not know what punishment was.

Oh yes, I forgot – no talking for two days. That's going to be hard.

Elizabeth was about to scold her son further, but a shout from Georgian in the medical room interrupted her.

"Brother! I think I've found something about the virus sprays!"

Darcy and Elizabeth hurried into the room where Georgiana awaited them, and saw that she had affixed more wires to Lydia's head.

"Information about the virus sprays from Lydia?" Elizabeth exclaimed.

"Yes! I was trying to see whether I could reverse the brainwashing's effects on your sister, and one of the electrodes fell off. When I tried to reattach it, I grazed the skin of her right earlobe – and it fell off! I was afraid that I had hurt her badly, but then I saw that it had been surgically done. And I found a computer chip there!" Georgiana motioned for her brother and Elizabeth to look at the display on the screen.

Blurry maps of Hawaii and Portugal were displayed.

"But there are no markings to show where the sprays are," Darcy murmured.

"Let's merge this file with the other encrypted file we found from the vault," Elizabeth said. She sat at the console and typed frantically, linking it to the other file which she had uploaded onto the main server.

Within moments, the files merged and the maps cleared up, with two purple dots appearing in Portugal and one in Hawaii.

Excited by the finding, Elizabeth contacted Colonel Morgan and Commander Brandon immediately, informing the ground forces of the exact ground locations of the brain-numbing torpedo sprays.

It took another tense two hours before all of the sprays had been located, identified, disabled and removed to safe locations, away from Earth's population, but it was all carried out with quiet efficiency, drawing little notice from people around the world. The threat of a mass panic had been avoided.

"That was close," Elizabeth murmured, as she massaged her sore neck.

"Let's get you to sleep," Darcy said softly, and kissed her cheek. He wrapped his hands around her waist while they monitored the progress of the operation in the medical room. "You've had a long two days. I don't want you overtired. We've got to think of Logan, though the young chap sometimes does not deserve it."

"But we haven't found any more details about Lady Catherine's transactions with Queen Thorpe yet," Elizabeth objected.

"My aunt has been arrested. She can't do anything yet except sit royally enclosed in that prison cell. Let's have some rest." He pulled her up from her seat and moved her out of the room. "Georgie, you should get some rest, too. Have the others continue the brain detoxing process for Lydia and Wickham."

"Aye, aye, Bro!" Georgiana said. "Though I'm not sure if it will do them any good. Their brains look very jumbled up. Perhaps I should get Caroline back and mix the three of their brains memories together. That would be fun!"

Darcy was shaken by Georgiana's laughter. *Had my little sister turned into a mad scientist? I hope it wasn't due to the influence of Sir Lewis.*

When Darcy and Elizabeth returned to their bedchamber in the palace, he pulled her into the spacious bathroom and removed their clothes efficiently. After adjusting the water to a comfortably warm temperature, he foamed up his hand and started massaging her shoulders.

"Hmm, that feels heavenly!" Elizabeth said, eyes half-closed.

He continued to massage her back, and kissed her softly while he did so. "Mrs. President, you deserve it. You cracked the encrypted files and saved hundreds of thousands of people. I don't even want to imagine what kind of poison Wickham had in those sprays."

"Perhaps something similar to what controls Lydia's brain," Elizabeth murmured. "When she attacked me, she said that she kills all Bennets, Darcys and Fitzwilliams."

"That would be scary, to have so many zombies determined to kill us and our families."

"Hmm. Remind me to talk to Georgiana tomorrow," she said in a tired mumble. "She should examine Lydia more thoroughly. Maybe there is something else that could lead to the discovery of Lord and Lady Matlock."

"You're right." Darcy nodded. "Maybe Georgie can check the composition of the torpedo, to see if she can find anything to help reverse Lydia's brain function."

"Hmm..." she said.

By the time Darcy finished drying her with towels, she had fallen asleep on her feet. He carried her to the bed, and they slept deeply.

***

When Darcy awoke and looked out at the vision pocket, it was bright and sunny. He raised his head to admire his wife.

Elizabeth was sleeping with a smile. She looked relaxed and glowing, despite the previous long hours. Her lips curled up at a teasing angle.

Pushing the blanket farther down, he revealed her slender neck and creamy shoulders. He liked the fact that Elizabeth was not pencil-thin. She had been curvy and womanly, even before she got pregnant, and therefore seemed much more 'real' to him than women like Caroline Bingley, who tried every possible way to be slim, even going to the length of surgically reducing their body fat. They were all bony, like skeletons, and all with similar features, like replicas. Their skin and muscles seemed starved for nutrients.

Unwilling to dwell any longer on the unpleasant topic of Miss Bingley, Darcy pulled the garment down slowly, exposing Elizabeth's creamy breasts. With the pregnancy, her aureoles had become enormous, and he considered the change in her figure to be incredibly sexy.

It was nature's proof of their love and affection for their children. He found it surprisingly spiritual to observe every single transformation of her body and emotions, throughout the past weeks. The process of childbearing was sacred, and the meaning behind it deeply significant. In this galaxy, every savage could reproduce, by natural or artificial means. But no matter what the method, if reproduction was based on love between the parties involved, it deserved to be respected.

With a dreamy smile, Darcy thought back on his acquaintance with Elizabeth, and their time together. In Hertfordshire, when he first met her, he had tried to resist her attraction and suppress his feeling. The constant warring within had made him look like a glowering bear, pacing angrily through social gatherings every time he met her. And, each time, he left the area with a heavy and depressed heart.

Not long thereafter, he had received her invitation to the mating capsule. How very exciting that had been! He still remembered how he had gazed at the card for ages, touching and feeling it. The words on the invitation had seemed to jump out at his eyes. At first, he wasn't sure if he should accept or not. The stakes were high. It wouldn't look good if he was caught using such an illegal establishment. But she yearned for him, or so he wanted to believe. He couldn't let the chance pass without finding out what she wanted. And so he made up his mind to discover what Elizabeth was about. Although he regretted it soon afterwards, his curiosity and her attraction finally won him over.

Darcy was shocked and a bit angered by her request that he give her a baby by using the insemination method. He felt hurt that she would tie him up and consider getting his sperm without his consent. From there, they had made love and, although it was beautiful, it was not truly a union of minds. She wasn't in love with him then, And his feelings had been tumultuous, too. He wasn't sure whether he was only infatuated with her or whether he loved her, a tiny bit.

Soon, they were freefalling onto Planet Hartfield, which was frightening and terrible. He felt helpless, unable to protect her and save their lives. Darcy thought that they might die together and be lost in the galaxy's black holes. Later, they were connected to Bingley for a brief moment. He had been feeling quite optimistic again, before they fell down into the Heart. It was like riding on a malfunctioning space ship; one minute he was on high and in control, and the next moment he was in a nose-dive, with the vessel spinning out of orbit.

What a coincidence that he had found his uncle, Sir Lewis, in the Heart. Those few weeks were both exciting and a time of despair. On the one hand, Darcy believed that he could feel her love for him starting to grow. He also felt more and more in love with her, as he discovered that she was strong and positive

Still, the constant fear of never returning to Planet Earth scared him. He didn't want to spend the rest of his life in a dark universe. There were times when he would succumb to depression, and his thoughts would spiral down. He blamed himself for suggesting that they exit the mating capsule and explore Hartfield, instead of awaiting their fate inside. He regretted dragging her down with him, to the centre of Hartfield.

At those times when he was tearing at himself emotionally, Elizabeth was able to bring him, back with her gentle and encouraging words. Although she experienced the same fears, distress and tortures, Darcy felt that she was much quicker to put them aside and concentrate on their daily activities. She would suggest that they make notes concerning the flora in the Heart, or the changes in atmospheric composition that they could feel. She appealed to his agricultural interest, to pull him away from the depressing thoughts and turn his focus outward.

It was wonderful to discover that Elizabeth had fallen pregnant. The wedding was solemn, respectful and memorable, and it went a long way toward lessening his hopelessness. Darcy knew by then that she loved him, but that it was not because of his wealth or physical appearance. After all, he had neither when he was in the Heart. He was just an ordinary man, with many jumbled emotional knots. He looked a sight, with long hair, outgrown beard, roughened skin and scraped muscles. No, Elizabeth loved him because of his character, and her trust and faith in him was priceless. He was enough for her, just as he was.

He had once been a proud man, not demonstrative about his feelings or appreciation. He sometimes looked down on people from the lower classes, like the Bennets. He had been taught to be that way by his family when he was young, and most of his wealthy and well-connected friends behaved like that, too. But the experience at the Heart stripped him to his bare essentials. Being the owner of Pemberley, the nephew of the Queen Immortal, one of the richest landlords, or one of the handsomest men on Planet Earth could do nothing to help him escape from the dark centre of Hartfield.

Only Elizabeth's encouragement, teasing, laughter and love had gotten him through the bleakest moments. And she had done all of that not because of his wealth, connections or position. She had been like a rock throughout the entire ordeal, all because of her love for him! And she had never asked for anything in return, no promise of jewels or property or prestige in the future.

Her unconditional love humbled him. Darcy wanted to make her proud, in return. He wanted to love her in the same way, to protect her, to share her worries and happiness every day, irrespective of her background or faults. He wanted to have children with her, and to grow old with her.

Fitzwilliam Darcy's glorious life and future would be forever linked to Elizabeth Bennet, this wonderful woman from a little place on Planet Earth.

He wondered, sometimes, what would have happened if he hadn't accepted Bingley's invitation to Hertfordshire. Would he still have met her? Would he still have the experience of loving someone fully and being loved in return? Life was truly amazing when he got to share it with his beloved Elizabeth.

Lowering his head, Darcy gave her a tender thank-you kiss on the mouth. Elizabeth blinked open her eyes and smiled groggily. Raising her hands, she wrapped them around his neck and returned his kiss passionately.

She nipped his lips and put her tiny tongue into his mouth. Her little hands moved from his neck to his spine. Every caress heated a burning trail on his body. He felt his arousal harden.

Sucking her sweet tongue, he moved his hands to palm her gorgeous breasts. To the accompaniment of her moans and groans, his fingers enjoyed the smooth texture of her skin and the hardened peaks.

As his thumbs rolled and brushed her nipples, he was delighted to feel her moving impatiently against his body. Her hips ground against his, and her legs stroked his thighs and calves.

"Are you feeling all right?" he asked huskily.

"I'll feel better when you come inside me."

He was ecstatic. He wanted more of her delicious body. His mouth abandoned her lips reluctantly and followed her womanly scent to her delectable earlobe. Elizabeth sighed loudly.

As her hands moved to his waist, his explorations took him farther. His mouth now drank in the sweet taste of her stunning breasts, while his palm found the bush at the juncture of her thighs.

She cried out and squirmed, as his teeth pulled her nipples to new heights and his fingers teased her sex. She was hot and wet. Her body thrust up aimlessly. When he rubbed her nub with decisive strokes, her hands gripped his butt cheeks fiercely.

Roll after roll, his tongue laved, suckled and tasted her enticing nipples. Up and down, his fingers stirred fire in her womanhood. Her scream became urgent and loud, but before she reached her climax, he moved on top of her and eased himself into her sultry body.

He strove to be slow, progressing inch by inch. His thick, hard cock wanted to savour every second of the sensation of duelling with her drenched, tight muscles. But she was extremely impatient. Her hands forced his bottom down toward her while her body jerked up to meet him. She seemed determined to push him over the edge as quickly as possible.

Darcy raised his head and groaned aloud before yielding to her demand and picking up the pace. Bracing himself, he pounded into her sizzling hot body again and again at wild speed. In the middle of his fanatic race up to Heaven, he heard her cry out in ecstasy. He drove hard into her sex for several more seconds, then reached his own shattering peak.

He collapsed onto her trembling form. Sweating and panting, they were unified, breathing as one. For a long time, they snuggled tightly together, without a word.

"Wow!" Elizabeth finally said.

He eased off of her body and brushed the curls from her sweaty forehead. "Was I too rough? Did I hurt you?"

She kissed his palm and said, "It was wonderful."

"I love you, my dearest, loveliest Elizabeth!"

"I love you, too," she murmured, resting her cheek on his shoulders.

And I love you both, Logan added.

"What are we to do with this unruly son?" Elizabeth murmured, and Darcy and she both ruefully shook their heads.

CHAPTER EIGHTEEN

In the next few days, the floating palace was moved to Pemberley so that President Mrs. Darcy could operate from there. It was the first time Elizabeth set her eyes on Pemberley, Darcy's beautiful home. She was awed by its natural beauty and homey feeling. Although she was busy with state affairs, she met with the staff there and settled in well.

Her family had returned to Hertfordshire, though her mother was reluctant to leave Lydia behind. But they could not do much for the brainwashed teenager except to wait while the palace's medical team worked on her. Since their arrest, the Bennets hadn't been back to their own home, so Mr. Bennet persuaded his wife to go back and wait for news, trusting that Elizabeth would take good care of her youngest sister.

Bingley had asked Jane to marry him, and they planned to marry in six months' time. The news was greeted with jubilation by their friends and the Bennets, though not by Caroline. She had gone missing and there was no record of her leaving Planet Earth. Privately, Charles believed that his sister would contact him when she ran out of the money needed to sustain her fashionable style of living.

The military was restoring order in every city. The people locked up by Prince Wickham – mainly noblemen and women, along with some others from the merchant and lower classes – were released. Compensation for those individuals was arranged. Over ten thousand people had been injured in the mere handful of weeks under the wicked prince's rule. Although the Queen Immortal had not been a good ruler, her suppression was less large-scale. Hospitals around Planet Earth were filled with injured people.

Elizabeth worked tirelessly with her two advisers to draft legislation to change the class system on Planet Earth. Once the restrictive legislation put in place by Catherine de Bourgh over the past 20 years had been repealed, and new legislation voted in, people would be allowed to engage in intimate relations, marriage and children with any person they chose.

The encrypted file from Lydia and the vault held another clue. Lord and Lady Matlock had not been sent to Hartfield, after all. It was a decoy that Prince Wickham had sprung onto the General. Instead, Richard's parents were locked up in Wickham's ancestral home in Ramsgate.

"Bloody Wickham! My parents are fine?" General Fitzwilliam asked Darcy with concern, upon hearing the latter's revelation about the Matlocks' whereabouts.

"They are fine. Just a few bruises and some malnutrition. The medical team is taking care of them."

"I'll strangle Wickham when I return. Wasted my time and effort by going to Hartfield," General Fitzwilliam cursed. "So, what other developments are there, on Earth?"

Darcy filled him in about the transfer of money from Lady Catherine's accounts to Queen Thorpe's.

"So you think there is something suspicious about Lady Catherine's signature?" the General asked.

"Yes, but I don't yet know the significance," Darcy murmured. "The legal proceeding to prosecute Lady Catherine is in process, but she is not opening up. We'll have to wait for the information from Galaxy Haven."

"Then our aunt will need to park her bum in that cell for a long time. I don't know who she wants to protect."

"Nor do I." Darcy shook his head. "Unless she has some fanatic supporters whom she trusts will stage a prison break for her."

"We'll watch her with our best bio-eye surveillance system. So, on a lighter note, how do you like being the First Bloke on Planet Earth?

"What first bloke?" Darcy scowled.

"Well, every successful woman must have a man behind her. Mrs. President Darcy no doubt requires a good man to take care of her clothes and cook for her while she rules over our beloved Planet for the time being."

"You're back to your idiotic self, Richard. I swear, you and Logan are like robotic clowns cast from the same mould."

"How is my favourite glowing nephew?"

"He's behaving better, since the disciplinary regime that we started after he hurt his mother accidentally. But he has been thick as thieves with Uncle Lewis. Both of them have been helping Georgiana to sort out the messed-up brains of Wickham and Lydia."

"How can Logan do that when Elizabeth is busy working on the Planet's affairs?"

"He mind-talks with Sir Lewis, over the computer. This is his favourite method of communication – to shut the parents out, I suspect." Darcy shook his head. "He's like a teenager now. A scary thought."

"Poor Darcy. At this rate, you will have to bear with Logan's mood twice. He'll have a real teenage rage when he reaches fifteen. Now, back to serious business, is there any progress with Caroline Wickham and Lydia?"

"Don't call him Caroline Wickham," Darcy protested with a shudder.

"Well, Prince Wickham has some of the elegant Miss Bingley's memory, and he's physically a woman now. I can't very well call him 'George Wickham' any more," Richard grinned. "After all, he wants to marry you – in an orange wedding dress, no less. He's very like Caroline, So I think it's a good name to call Prince Wickham, from now on."

"Brother! Brother!" Georgiana's sudden cry interrupted the General and Darcy.

"What is it, Georgie?" Richard said.

"Wickham's mind seems to be cleared, but he's talking nonsense," Georgiana said breathlessly, her communication from the medical room broadcasting over Richard and Darcy's conversation.

"Wickham has regained his solitary memory and yet he's still illogical?" Richard murmured. "How typical of him."

"I'll come over," Darcy said.

"Connect me again when you're in the medical room," Richard requested.

When Darcy arrived, he found that Elizabeth and Sir Lewis were there, too. Georgiana connected Richard to her computer console.

"What's happening?" Sir Lewis asked eagerly, eyeing Wickham with disdain.

Wickham appeared to be sleeping rather peacefully, but Georgiana rewound the earlier surveillance footage of the medical wing. "I was working in Lydia's room when I heard some loud cries. They seemed to be coming from Wickham's quarters, so I hurried in to investigate. He mumbled a few nonsensical sentences and then swooned. When I roused him to check on him, he was vicious and angry, very much like himself when he tried to hurt me in Matlock. There was no confusion between himself and Caroline Bingley. Then he became tired and fell asleep again."

"But why were you alarmed? Why did you call us in here?" Elizabeth asked with a frown.

"Well, as I was preparing to go back to Lydia, I thought about the strange words that burst from Wickham when he woke, just now. I couldn't recall them precisely, so I rewound the surveillance footage to listen to them again. I couldn't make sense of what he said but it seems to be related to a murder – perhaps that of Queen Thorpe."

Elizabeth and Darcy gasped.

Oh, the bad Princess Caroline Wickham was involved in that, too? Logan speculated. *Evil woman-man!*

"I'll let you watch the tape," Georgian said. "I'm not 100% sure what he meant."

The footage showed Wickham thrashing and pulling at the restraints that held him down on the bed. He cried out, "We can't do this...we can't...it's murder! I don't want to lose you. You'll be fed to the aliens...I love you. We don't need this...money...power... Please don't make me...I don't want...to do this."

"So, Wickham was controlled by a woman," Richard said. "But who? Who was it who planned a murder?"

"His girlfriend?" Darcy murmured.

"It sounds as if she pressured Wickham to kill," Sir Lewis said. "But we don't know if it's related to Queen Thorpe's murder or not. Did he have a lot of girlfriends, through the years?"

Darcy nodded, and Richard added, "Wickham was a charmer. He had so many girlfriends that I lost count."

"If this murder is not related to Queen Thorpe, I won't involve myself personally," Elizabeth said. "But I will hand him over to the police. Can you work on his memory, Georgiana? To have him reveal more?"

"Maybe you can use hypnosis," Sir Lewis pondered.

"Psychologists in ancient times liked to use that method to persuade people to reveal their darkest secrets," Georgiana said. "But I'm not skilled in it."

"We still have Galaxy Haven to rely on, concerning Lady Catherine's case," Elizabeth said. "I will give permission for a medical expert to hypnotise Wickham, in order to probe for more information about this murder."

***

Two days later, the General returned. First, he visited his parents, who were in good health.

While he was in a meeting with Mrs. President, the alarm was raised in the high security prison.

"Colonel Morgan, you have a situation?" General Fitzwilliam asked, via the computer console.

"Aye, sir. It's Wickham! He broke free from the medical room while he was under hypnosis, and he is reported to be at the prison, where he has forced his way into Lady Catherine's jail cell. Your aunt has taken him hostage, and she is demanding to have a warship prepared to take her to Galaxy Haven."

"I'll come right over. Alert the hostage negotiator," General Fitzwilliam directed.

When he left, Elizabeth followed at his heels, despite his protest. By the time they arrived at the concourse of the prison compound, Darcy, Sir Lewis and Georgiana were also there.

"Elizabeth, you shouldn't be here," Darcy said anxiously, and embraced her shoulders, pulling her out of harm's way.

"I won't go near the action," she assured him. "But I want to oversee the situation and determine what can be done," she replied. "How did you get here so quickly?"

"Sir Lewis, Georgiana and I were in the medical room, and we heard Wickham subduing the doctor who was hypnotising him. Even then, we couldn't stop him fast enough. He grabbed some laser daggers and reacted like a man possessed, injuring anyone who tried to block his way. We followed him here."

"Catherine, release Wickham," Sir Lewis exclaimed. "You can't get away. Your captive will be on trial soon. The guards won't mind if you shoot him. It would simply save us the bother of a legal procedure."

"Don't you 'Catherine' me!" Lady Catherine hissed, her eyes red with anger.

"Mother, please release me!" Wickham muttered. His voice was low, as his throat was being held tightly by Lady Catherine. He sounded shaky, but everyone in the concourse heard his startling words.

"What?" Sir Lewis cried out. "Is he your love child, from before you married me?"

"Shut up, George," Lady Catherine chastised Wickham.

"We don't need this...money...power...Mom. Please, let us go away," Wickham pleaded, a single tear dropping from his eyelashes. "I love you. Please!"

"I don't want you anymore!" Lady Catherine sputtered. Her face turned bright red, as if she might burst a vein. "You are no longer my lovely little boy. You've turned into a stupid woman. Like Caroline Bingley, you're just trying to use your body to seduce men now. You've no guts or strength! I don't love you, not any more"

Elizabeth pressed her hand to her mouth. "I'm going to be sick," she murmured to her husband. "Does this mean that Lady Catherine has been sleeping with Wickham, who is her SON?"

The laser dagger that Lady Catherine was holding traced a bloody line down Wickham's cheek. He yelped in pain.

"I've done everything you asked, Mother!" Wickham continued, his tone soft and tender. "I've been a good boy. Can't we leave Planet Earth and start afresh somewhere else? I've transferred some money away, enough to last our lifetime."

"Shut up!" Lady Catherine said. "Richard, where is my warship? If I don't have it within the next few minutes, I'm going to tear Wickham's heart open." As if to demonstrate her point, she slid the dagger along Wickham's womanly left breast.

"Please don't hurt me. I don't want to be fed to the aliens, like Lady Catherine." Tears ran down from Wickham's face now. He was sobbing like a little boy.

"I told you to shut up!" Lady Catherine tried to cover his mouth, to prevent him from divulging any more information, but he continued to whimper.

"I don't understand," Darcy whispered to his wife. "What did Wickham mean about Lady Catherine being fed by aliens?"

I don't understand it either, Dad, Logan jumped in. *Isn't that Lady Catherine standing right there, threatening her son, Princess Wickham?*

Elizabeth suddenly linked the missing pieces together and thought of another possibility. Gasping, she called out loudly, "Mrs. Wickham, you cannot get away with killing Lady Catherine and Queen Thorpe!"

Lady Catherine swung her head in Elizabeth's direction, and narrowed her eyes menacingly. "It's all your fault! You're nothing but a country upstart with no connections or wealth. Why did you have to want a child with Darcy, who should have been far out of your reach? If you had stayed within your class and sphere, none of this would have come out! I would still be the Queen Immortal, and George would still be my handsome, lovely boy!"

"You made your son kill Lady Catherine," Elizabeth said sternly, depending on her hunch. "He was only 12 years old, at the time. How could you live with knowing that you turned your young son into a murderer?"

"I was ten," Wickham said in a trembling voice, and closed his tear-filled eyes.

"It was a great scheme!" Lady Catherine – no, Mrs. Wickham – laughed out loud. "George killed Lady Catherine and Queen Thorpe, all by himself. It has nothing to do with me."

"But you ordered me to do it," Wickham retorted, as if unable to hide the secret any more. "You said Lady Catherine was a stupid old cow who didn't know how to make the most of her position in society. You said that skimming off a few people here and there wouldn't make her almighty."

"No, you tried to please me," his mother protested, her hand tightening on Wickham's throat again. "You said you wanted to make me rich and powerful – the Goddess on Planet Earth, commanding people, deciding their fate, and who they could have sex with, and when they could have children. An orderly society, with less population, all under the control of a strong woman like me. You arranged for Lewis to be dumped on Hartfield. You lured Catherine to the carnivorous aliens. And you killed Thorpe when she wanted more money and tried to break away from my control. You did everything for me, because you love me. I didn't ask you to. You're just a clinging little man, begging for my attention."

"No! You betrayed me!" Wickham yelled. He grabbed his mother's arm, and it seemed to free his voice. "I love you, Mother, but you have taken on lovers. When I was injured by Georgiana, you turned a cold shoulder to me. You said you wouldn't allow me back into your bed until after I'd mastered the skill of pleasing women with my tongue and hands. You betrayed me! I hate you!" Wickham suddenly twisted in his mother's grasp. "No, I love you, Mother! I will never let you go. You're mine forever! Only mine!" he cried, and thrust his laser dagger into Mrs. Wickham's stomach.

Mrs. Wickham cried out in pain, her eyes widening with fear.

The guards, who had stood frozen by the brawling of the two crazy women, finally regained their wits and dashed forward to yank Wickham away from his victim. Mrs. Wickham dropped to the floor, contorted in pain.

"Call the doctor!" Elizabeth instructed.

"And take Wickham to a restraining cell!" General Fitzwilliam added.

But it was too late for Mrs. Wickham, killed by her own son, whom she had groomed to be a killer.

EPILOGUE

After observing the emotional outbursts and the bloody scene, Elizabeth felt drained and disgusted. Her husband persuaded her to take a rest, and she entrusted the clean-up to the General.

A few hours later, Darcy came into their room and found her awake.

"How are you feeling, Elizabeth?" He lowered his head and kissed her mouth tenderly.

"Tired and horrified." She drew him down to lie beside her. "Did you suspect any of this?"

He hugged her tightly. "No, never."

"Tell me more about his family," she entreated. "I want to understand."

"His father, Reginald Wickham, was an excellent assistant to my father. He asked my father to stand as godfather when young Wickham was born. My father liked George a lot. Reginald died when George was just 5 years old, and so my father offered to take care of the boy and his mother, Daisy. When Daisy was found dead, five years later, we all felt very sorry for George, but he seemed to change then. He didn't seem to enjoy playing with Richard and me, after that, and we assumed that his mother's death had affected him badly.

When we went to Cambridge together, George became a womaniser, charming and seducing a lot of women, and he gambled and drank like no tomorrow. It was as if he hated living and wanted to exist in the dark. I didn't like his way at all. But I couldn't bring myself to mention it to my father. I didn't want to break his heart."

"No wonder he hated himself, if he killed Lady Catherine for his mother. Why did he suddenly reveal everything when he was held at dagger point by Mrs. Wickham?"

"The doctor who was hypnotising him says that George had been opening up to him about what happened when he was ten years old. Wickham was probably still under the influence of the hypnotism when he broke into the prison. After the attack, the doctor worked on him again, in the presence of the General and several guards. I was there, too, to observe. Do you want me to tell you the gist of it or would you rather watch the recording? It's not a pretty revelation."

Elizabeth sat up. "I'll watch the recording. It's better that I know everything, in case there is any issue concerning his trial."

Darcy called up the footage of Wickham under hypnosis, in the prison. Princess Wickham was strapped onto a bed, legs and hands bound.

"Think back in time, Wickham. You are ten years old. Your mother, Daisy, says she loves you. She wants you to help her to become rich and wealthy. What does she want you to do?"

"Mother wants me to lure the old cow to the vessel where the vicious aliens are staying," Wickham murmured. "And so that's what I do."

"How do you manage it?"

"I tell Lady Catherine that her daughter Anne has wandered off and gone there. So she goes there to find Anne. But three fearsome aliens from Planet Black are staying there."

"Does she go alone?" Richard interjects, guiding Wickham to reveal everything.

"Yes, I tell her to hurry, that I will call the guards for her."

"And what happens when she arrives?"

"Mother gave me some strange drugs to put into the food of the aliens, to trigger their flesh-eating appetite, about half an hour earlier. When Lady Catherine appears, she is gobbled up by the three hungry aliens. Even her bones are eaten." Wickham laughed, a horrible sound.

Elizabeth swallowed hard at hearing the viciousness in Wickham's voice.

"And what do you do?"

"Then Mother goes into surgery with Uncle Collins."

"Uncle Collins?"

"Yes, Norman Collins. Commander William Collins's father," Wickham said, and snickered.

"Why does your mother need to do that?"

"Uncle Collins is a plastic surgeon. He changes Mother into Lady Catherine on that day. She rests for a month or so, healing, before she reappears. It coincides with Sir Lewis's disappearance, so everyone thinks that Lady Catherine's heart is broken and that she doesn't want to be seen in public. He also finds a body which we bury as my mother's. But I hate him, because Collins forces Mother to sleep with him."

Elizabeth shook her head at those revelations. Mrs. Wickham had been a very calculating woman, and Collins no better!

"But what about Sir Lewis? Your mother doesn't want him killed?" Richard continued.

"Mother likes Sir Lewis, but he's in love with Lady Anne. No, she doesn't want him killed. She arranges for him to be dumped somewhere. I don't know where. I'm just ten years old at the time. She says that if he changes his mind about Lady Anne, she may release him from his torture."

On the recording, Elizabeth could see Sir Lewis's disgusted expression.

"And Queen Thorpe? How does she come into the scheme?" Richard pursued.

"As Uncle Collins's mistress, before she married the King. That stupid doctor told her what he had done, in his sleep, And so she blackmails Mom," Wickham sputtered angrily.

"But your mother doesn't want to harm her, at first? Queen Thorpe holds your mother's secret for twenty years."

"Yes, Mother admires Thorpe. She says she likes women who treat men like dirt. She says she's happy being the Genesis Director. She has enough wealth and power, especially since Thorpe is not the most attentive ruler and allows Mother to control everything, behind the scenes."

"What happens two years ago?"

"Thorpe wants more money. She's fallen in love with a pretty boy and wants to lavish more money on him," Wickham said, scowling. "So she tells Mother to give her more money. But Mother is sick of her pathetic attitude, all to please this young man. So she asks me to put Thorpe to sleep." He smiled smugly.

"Why doesn't your Mother allow you to go through surgical procedure, when you are hurt by Georgiana?" Richard continued.

"She says she doesn't like me to be with other women. She says I'm hers, alone, and so it's good that I'm a eunuch. This way, I can only please her, from now on." Wickham's face contorted with conflicting emotions.

"And yet you want to be in control over your mother?" Sir Lewis suggested.

"Yes, I don't like her doting on Darcy. She's growing to behave like the real Catherine de Bourgh. That's why I put her into a coma. I want to invade and occupy Planet Hartfield for her so that, when she wakes up, I'll be the only man for her, the most powerful man on Planet Earth. I'll have eliminated everyone who dares to go against my mother's wishes, including the Bennets, the Darcys and the Fitzwilliams! I will be King Immortal, ruling for thousands of years to come. I'll live forever! People will bow down and kiss my feet…" Wickham's crazy shriek continued.

Darcy switched off the recording and embraced Elizabeth tightly.

"Wickham is sick," she commented.

He nodded. "His mother shaped him and turned him into a maniac."

Elizabeth pressed her hands on her belly. "We have to teach Logan well. I want him to be compassionate and fair to people from all walks of life."

"Yes." Darcy kissed her softly. "Wealth comes from happiness of mind. Together, we will raise our son to be a happy young man, full of life."

***

Eight years passed.

The Queen Immortal's rule was over. The wicked Princess Wickham served her sentence in jail. General Fitzwilliam ruled Planet Earth for three terms. He had become the most eligible bachelor on Earth, with women fawning over him all the time. He became good friends with Commander Knightley, on Planet Hartfield, and was subjected to the endless match-making efforts of Knightley's wife, Emma.

Caroline Bingley was never heard from again. Her brother was sad about this from time to time, but he had a happy marriage with Jane, and they had three lovely children.

Sir Lewis had returned to Rosings with his daughter, Anne, and lived there quietly.

The Darcys were blessed with four children: Justin, Alex, Eva and Max Darcy. They all had well-developed brain function, thanks to the radioactive dates Darcy and Elizabeth consumed in the Heart.

Do you wonder what became of Logan Darcy?

He changed his name to Justin Darcy!

A few days before his birth, eight years earlier, he had mind-talked to his parents, requesting a change of name.

Mom, I don't want to be called Logan when I'm born, Logan said grumpily.

Elizabeth was resting on her bed, taking a maternity leave from her presidential duties. Work had begun on arranging the next presidential election, but Elizabeth had declined to participate. Instead, she was encouraging General Fitzwilliam to campaign for the post.

"You're quite restless lately," Elizabeth murmured.

"Yes, why did you want to change your name?" Darcy asked his son as he massaged his wife's shoulders. She was quite large now, just days from giving birth.

Aunt Lydia was browsing galaxynet yesterday. She found out that 'Logan' means 'hollow!' I don't want to be a hollow man! their son complained.

Lydia's brainwashing couldn't be reversed, but Georgiana did manage to erase her killer memory. Lydia returned to Longbourn but had to re-learn everything from scratch, like a baby. Logan enjoyed teaching his aunt to read and write, via computer link.

"But you said Sir Lewis wanted you to have this name, and that you wanted to honour his wishes," Elizabeth reminded him.

Sir Lewis dotes on me. He will be happy even if I choose another name, Logan argued.

"I've never heard of a baby giving himself a name," Darcy objected, and shook his head.

Well, some parents are insane, giving their kids weird names. Who wants to be called Apple or Sunday at school? I don't want to be teased, he continued to protest.

Elizabeth sighed. "What do you want to be named, then?"

Justin Darcy would be cool, Logan said proudly.

"Why Justin?" Darcy asked.

You two said you want me to be fair and compassionate. 'Fair' is 'just.' So Justin is cool, Logan said.

Darcy and Elizabeth looked at each other and nodded, deciding to let their unborn son decide his own name, rather than argue with him. In this teenage mood, it could have been a stalemate for weeks.

Justin Darcy was born, healthy, two days later. Besides a big head and advanced intelligence, his physical being was like that of any normal baby. His face wore a big grin when he was born, because he didn't tell his parents that he liked some ancient singers from the 21st century and wanted to be named after one of them. He had simply found a good argument to present to his parents.

His younger brothers and sister all chose their own names before they were born, thanks to the mind talk from their older brother. Darcy and Elizabeth had their hands full, shaping the characters of their children and raising them as upstanding citizen of Planet Earth. Their argument about character faults in the mating capsule was a concern of the distant past!